THE MEASURE OF
A MAN

THE MEASURE OF A MAN

Sunday Afternoons in Small-Town America

Continuing the Award Winning Dancing Deer Story with Book Three

Ron Lambert

Copyright © 2012 by Ron Lambert

Published in the United States by:

Printers Guild Publishing House, llc

425 Spring Street, Suite 101
Columbus, Texas 78934-2461
(979) 732-2962   Fax (979) 733-0015
www.printersguildpublshing.com

Library of Congress Control Number: 2013914818

ISBN 978-0-9855083-4-0

Contents

The Measure of a Man is a work of Fiction

Except for some historical personages the names, characters, and incidents of the story are used fictitiously and do not represent any actual person or event.

Some of the towns, cities, or geographic localities are real. An interested reader might be able to find Lee Mountain, the Buffalo River, the Illinois Bayou, the Big Piney, Moccasin Gap, or even Little Creek's water crossing. Eudy's Drug and Fountain might be harder.

The author grew up in a small rural community and saw wonder in all living things. He wrote this story using the hazy remembrances of a child's fertile imagination and sheer luck.

Trademarks

Cover

Art from Shutterstock.com

CHAPTER 1 – NEW YORK CITY
May, 1945

Faye Spencer and Dancing Deer's chief of police arrived with two suitcases, a make-up bag, and a manuscript. No one knew they were coming. No one was at the train station to greet them when they arrived. No one offered a ride to a hotel; there weren't any hotel reservations anyway. They left Dancing Deer with Chief W.W. Wainwright's life savings and the novel Faye wrote while being held for ransom by a murderer.

No one in Dancing Deer could remember another double homicide happening in their sleepy little Arkansas town. The citizens were not prepared. Three months earlier, in February, someone smothered Raylene Carlisle, a high-class prostitute, and shot a drifter outside Raylene's apartment building. Bill Potter, the richest man in town and owner of the town's bank and recently opened Ritz Grand Hotel, Ballroom, and Bistro Restaurant, was charged.

A few days into Bill's trial a hand reached out from a dark alleyway and snatched Faye. a reporter for the *Marsden County Meteor* and thought to be romantically involved with Potter. Faye Spencer disappeared in the clutches of a desperate man. For Faye's release her abductor demanded thirty thousand dollars. While Bill struggled to round up the money, Faye wrote a story about the murders as she understood them. She had a plausible scenario. When her facts became sparse or her prose boring, she liberally injected bits of humor and fantastic fight scenes.

Faye escaped. The authorities were now looking for her kidnapper, but they considered it a second crime not linked in any direct way to the murders. The county released Bill and issued a warrant for the arrest of their new suspected perpetrator—the county sheriff. With the town in a turmoil and the district attorney blaming his chief of police for bumbling the case against Potter, Faye Spencer and Chief of Police W.W. Wainwright escaped to find a publisher. They planned on coming back to a hero's welcome, with a best-seller under their belts, and wads of cash stuffed in their pockets.

"We need a room. I think we'll be here a couple of weeks. You got one with a sitting area?"

"I'm sorry, sir. We have no vacancies. The boys have started coming home and they get priority."

"No rooms available in the great city of New York? Would you check to see if any of your buddies down the street have a vacancy?"

"I'm sorry sir. Every one I'm aware of is full." The desk-clerk picked up an envelope of papers and started thumbing through. He looked up to see the man and pretty woman still standing at his counter. "You might try one of the shelters."

Dejected the two weary travelers walked to a settee and sat down. "Okay, W.W. what do we do now?"

"Relax, Faye. I've got a sister living in Queens. She'll put us up until I find a place. I can't believe they're all full."

Chief Wainwright's sister, Glenda, was thrilled. She had a guest bedroom and needed the company. Her husband had died fighting the Japanese in the Philippines and she was lonely. Besides, it had been four years since she'd seen her older brother.

While changing the bed linens with W.W.'s sister, Faye said, "You're sure this is okay? I mean, we didn't call or anything."

"I don't think Wayne has ever called before showing up. Sure it's okay. I wouldn't have it any other way. I've got this spare bedroom and plenty of linens and towels and, if you need anything during the day, I'll be downstairs in my shop."

Glenda lived on the floor above her beauty salon. She promised to fix coffee for them the next morning and let Faye know there were plenty of groceries in the cupboard and icebox for their breakfast.

Faye considered her new predicament. To this point, she and W.W. had not had intimate relations—they were just friends. Of course he wanted more, but she had managed to keep him at arm's length till now.

Chief Wainwright sat in his brother-in-law's rocker listening to the radio. In a few minutes he'd find out if he got to sleep in the same bed as the beautiful Faye Spencer or on the couch in the living room. He hadn't said anything to his sister. He thought he'd let the women sort out the particulars and let him know his situation.

Before long his sister came in and said, "Wayne, she sure is pretty. But she's half a foot taller than you. I suppose you're not married since she doesn't have a ring, and you introduced her using her maiden name. Are you engaged?"

"Not yet. Thought we'd do the honeymoon first."

"I can see you've still got your sense of humor. See you in the morning. Come down to the shop after you get dressed, we have a lot of catching up to do."

Wayne Winchell Wainwright turned off the radio and picked up a magazine. The suspense was killing him. Will I, or won't I?

Thirty minutes later, Faye walked into the living room. "Do you snore?"

CHAPTER 2 – THE HOTSHOTS

Let's see, if I let Carlos play short and his cousin Alito play second, then I've got a good double-play combination and two pretty good hitters. Julius Mosivido pondered the possibilities of putting together a troupe of barnstormers. Licking the point of his pencil, he scratched out the name he'd originally put down for shortstop.

I'll show him. Didn't think it was a good idea. Not the right time. Sore arm. The kid had a basketful of excuses. Carlos is past his prime, but he's kept fit and only gives up a little range. He'll make a better shortstop anyway, more dependable.

Julius shifted to the problem every beginning entrepreneur struggles with—capital. He'd lost his job building ships. Caught drinking on the job, his supervisor said it was the third and last time. So Julius went looking for his kid brother and found him pimping the lower east-side.

That boy's loaded, has a wad of money big enough to choke a horse. Says he's not interested in barnstorming. With eight women working the streets, he's bought a half interest in a joint filled every night with workers from the box factory.

Julius had heard men and women worked three shifts to build the wooden boxes used to hold ammunition. Some boxes held coiled belts used by machine guns, some large projectiles with fins, others would eventually hold heavier rounds for the Sherman tanks. The people worked around the clock to build and ship those boxes to other plants for filling and sending to war. The nightclub provided the male workers with a little relaxation before they took it on home to their old ladies.

The joint was called "The Topless Wonder" and the boy planned on making so much money, between running the girls and the booze, he told Julius, he would soon have enough to cash in and retire to their native Cuba.

"How much you need, Julius?" Just like that. I had told him I needed some front money to get everything rolling and he reached into his pocket, pulled out a leather wallet on a gold chain, and said, "How much you need, Julius?" I wanted five hundred, but quickly changed gears and drove away with three grand.

After getting the money, Julius had his beginning capital problem solved and started recruiting players. He couldn't believe his good fortune. He was actually going to field a ball team. He still needed a catcher and a pitcher, but the pieces were slowly falling into place. Soon he'd head west and play games in every small town that could field a team.

"James Paul, if you don't get a job and start helping out, I'm gonna haul your ass down to the Army recruiting office and ship you off myself. I don't care if you do have a perforated eardrum. You just lie around in bed while I go cleaning other people's houses. It ain't right. Your dad worked himself to the grave so we'd have a nice place to live and food on the table. Now he's gone, I'm holding down two jobs to keep the creditors from taking what we got, and I find you sneaking money outta my purse. That's the last straw. You go to that box factory today and see if they're hiring. Boy, you got to help out—or get out."

James Paul slipped on his shoes, stuck two pieces of bacon in a biscuit and walked out the front screened door. He might have to get a job. She might mean it this time and he sure as hell didn't want to join the Army.

At the box factory, James Paul was ushered into a long room that doubled as a cafeteria and was filled with small tables. He was told to fill out a form and to ring a bell when finished. He thought he might take it with him and bring it back the next day, but decided that would be wasting two days, so he filled out the questions he wanted to answer and rang the bell.

"Follow me. The shipping supervisor told me to bring him anyone showing up who looked like he was strong enough to lift a hundred pounds. Boy, this might be your lucky day."

James Paul didn't want a job, he just wanted to apply. "I can't lift a hundred pounds. You think I'm a mule or something?"

14

"No, I think you're a strong young man who needs to stay out of the Army. Working here will accomplish that for you."

"How much you pay?"

"I think the stacker gets a dollar a pallet, maybe more."

Fifteen minutes later James Paul met the foreman, who took him to the warehouse and told him to start stacking the boxes traveling along a looped conveyer belt. A platform at his feet held forty-eight stacked boxes. After positioning the boxes, James Paul was told to tie them together, so when they were transported by a fork-lift to the cargo bed of a truck, they'd stay bundled. At the end of the day James Paul had stacked eight pallets and his back was killing him. When he sat down at the end of his shift, his biceps quivered.

"After a couple of weeks, those muscles will toughen up and your job will be a piece of cake."

James Paul looked into the rheumy eyes of the fellow worker who had shown him the proper way to stack and then to tie the stacks together. "I think I need a job requiring a little more brain and a little less muscle."

"You'll have to work into one like that. Let me buy you a drink. You worked hard today. You deserve a little refreshment."

"When do we get paid?"

"At the end of next week. Ain't you ever had a job?"

"Nope, just played ball and chased women."

"Ha, ha, you'll fit right in. I ain't never seen anyone work so hard and get so little done. When you figure things out, you'll be putting the rest of us to shame."

"How about the guy driving the fork-lift? Think maybe there might be an opening there?"

"Hardly. And you with no seniority wouldn't get it if there was."

"What about the supervisor? How do you get a job like that?"

"You really are funny. I'm gonna enjoy working with you. Tell me about your ball playing and about those women."

"Why do your friends call you 'Spider?'"

"Well, Baby-Doll, cause I'm skinny with long arms and legs. When I curl up with a woman I completely wrap around her until she can't move. Course, she don't want to move—except to squirm a little when I start nibbling on her neck."

The man called Spider motioned to the barkeep for more drinks for him and his new lady-friend.

"Stick out your tongue."

"You want to see how long it is?"

"No. I want to see if the damned thing's dripping honey."

"Baby-Doll, you are too funny. I'll let you see my tongue if you'll let me see if you're as big breasted as you're advertising."

"Maybe later. How about you and me shooting some pool?"

Three racks later and with six more drinks under his belt, the man called Spider had a hard time standing. Baby-Doll racked for his playing adversary.

After playing one game with Baby-Doll, Spider had been challenged by a tall, husky bear of a man with an agenda. "Let's play one more, Spider. If you win, I'll give you this crisp one-hundred-dollar bill and forget the twenty you're down. And if you lose, you got to pitch two games for my baseball team."

"I love to play ball. You know, I can throw a curve that starts out at the batter and, when he hits the dirt, the ball sweeps across the plate down the center. Damn thing must break a foot or more."

"That's what I've been told."

"I'd probably play on your team without losing this game of pool, but I think I'll take your money anyway."

Julius handed Spider the ball and said, "I'll even let you break."

"Baby-Doll, come over here and help me stand. I'm swaying so much I'm gonna miss the damn cue-ball." Spider tried to make a bridge, but somehow his fingers wouldn't let the cue slide through. "Any way we can make that two-hundred dollars?"

"Yeah, but if you lose, you got to play all week. I got a game scheduled in Martin on Tuesday, another in Finks on Thursday, and two more down the road a piece on Saturday and Sunday."

"Hey, mister, you need a catcher?"

"Depends. You any good?"

"Caught the 'Big Train' in an exhibition once."

Spider held out his stick for Baby-Doll to chalk. "The Big Train throws awfully hard, but a curve like mine would wear you out with all the trips you'd have to make to the backstop."

"I think they call you Spider cause you're so disagreeable."

"You might be right, kid, but after I win this two hundred, our mark might not have enough left to play you."

"Just shoot the damn balls."

"Baby-Doll, you got to move that arm. My stick's hitting it on the back stroke."

Spider broke and pocketed the five-ball. "Guess I'm the little ones. Baby-Doll, let's go to the other side. I want to shoot the three." With Baby-Doll's arms wrapped around his waist, propping him up, Spider made two more balls before missing and leaving Julius corner-hooked.

"Damn. You're the luckiest man I've ever played." Julius scratched.

Spider ran the rest of his balls and banked the eight in the side pocket. Baby-Doll let go long enough to retrieve his winnings and, when she came back, Spider was asleep under the table.

James Paul walked up and said, "I don't play a good stick. How 'bout you just pay me to catch your four games. Say twenty each?"

"I can only start you with ten a game, but if you'll help drive the bus I'll throw in a little extra. Here, help me load Spider in the back."

CHAPTER 3 – SHERIFF SHODTOE

"Where the hell is that kid?" Sheriff Shodtoe stirred his coffee and fidgeted in his seat. He picked up the menu and started looking for something different from the breakfast he'd had there the morning before and the one the morning before that.

"Oh, man. Sherman, look at this. They have your picture in the paper. Says here Marsden County issued a warrant for your arrest. Sherman, they've started a state-wide manhunt."

"Let me see that."

Raymond Henderson was Sherman's cousin and on Dancing Deer's city police force. Sherman was Arkansas' Marsden County Sheriff. Raymond handed Sherman the newspaper and looked around to see if any of the other customers were reading this morning's paper.

"Sherman, we got to go."

The sheriff looked at his picture, then up at his cousin. He quickly placed two dollar bills on the table and, pulling his cowboy hat down low, walked briskly to the door.

"I got to get me some aviator glasses and grow a mustache or a beard. How come Johnson hasn't found that kid? If we could locate him I'd haul his ass in and set the record straight. They don't want me, they want Evan Bonds. I didn't kill Raylene and that bum, he did."

"I know, but the district attorney doesn't. Mr. Jellico painted a convincing picture with you as the villain and his client as wrongly accused. Bill Potter was found not guilty and now every police officer in Dancing Deer is looking for you. And now they've got everyone in the state looking as well. We'll be lucky to get our things and get over the state line before we're caught."

"I know. You think I don't know that? You go up to the room; I'll stay with the car. Just stuff everything in the suitcases. Don't sort it out, don't fold nothing. Use a pillowcase if you have to. Just get in, get our stuff, and get out. We paid a week in advance so you don't even have to check out. Quiet as a mouse, we'll slip into Missouri."

"Sherman, does it look like there are more cars than usual in the parking lot?"

"Hell, yeah. Skip the clothes. We'll pick up that nephew of ours and get out of town. Buy new stuff in the show-me state."

Sheriff Sherman Shodtoe shifted the car into reverse and backed out of his parking space. A police cruiser pulled up behind and another in front. Several police officers jumped out with pistols drawn and pointing at the two fugitives. A tall lanky cowboy strolled over to the sheriff's car. Through the rolled down window he said, "You fellers heading somewhere?"

At police headquarters the two law enforcement officers just recently listed as wanted for questioning were fingerprinted and their pictures taken before being placed in adjacent cells.

"I'm telling you, I'm not the man you want. I want to see your police chief—a Mr. Bonds, a Mr. Benjamin Bonds." Sherman looked over his cell: three concrete block walls and ceiling, with a concrete slab floor, and a toilet and cot—both bolted to the floor. Primitive, but habitable.

"I'll tell him, but I think right now he's on the line to some people in Dancing Deer."

From the next cell came a soft, "Don't make any more trouble than you have to. Don't try to bribe him or anything. If we can get back to Dancing Deer we might be able to straighten this out, but if you tell Chief Bonds his son killed those two people and you've been charged with the crime because no one but you knows his son did it, then they may never know. He could say we escaped or tried to escape. Damnit, Sherman, this one time use your head."

CHAPTER 4 – PUBLISHERS

Faye dressed in the only clean, pressed garment she had. After she got things rolling on the book she thought she'd better address the dirty clothes issue. Picking up her new valise containing the manuscript of her book, she left Chief Wainwright lying in bed snoring loud enough to make children cry.

From the telephone directory Faye copied down the names, addresses, and telephone numbers of a dozen publishing houses. Glenda had prepared coffee before descending to her shop for the day, so Faye fixed a cup and sat down to plan her excursion into the big city. In the adjacent chair she carefully placed her treasure.

Faye was proud of her novel. She thought it an outstandingly good read even though she didn't solve it like Jellico and his team of detectives. Still, being locked up, she was not privy to the facts as they were and, since she had made it a work of fiction, she could make up whatever scenario seemed appropriate. Just put in enough twists, a few red herrings, sprinkle in a liberal assortment of clues, and populate it with colorful characters. That was her recipe for a blockbuster best-seller.

She had toyed with the idea of waking W.W. but decided against it. He'd be up on his own in a short while. Because they were traveling on his money, she thought she'd be nice and let him sleep. He'd had a hard time sleeping on the train. The stress was starting to show in his eyes. Maybe, when she got back, he will have found them rooms. Faye called a taxi.

Picking up the newspaper from the front stoop, she walked briskly to the waiting cab. Three hours later she decided to find a place to eat and re-think her strategy. She'd been to four publishers and had not made it past the receptionist. Either they were not acquiring novels at this time, they were not accepting work from un-agented authors, or they were too busy to see someone without an appointment. This latter excuse was promising until she was told they weren't making appointments.

Chief Wainwright descended the stairs to his sister's salon. She was putting the finishing touches to an elderly woman's permanent.

"So where's Faye?" asked Glenda as she took off her client's cotton wrap.

"Don't know. Thought she might be down here." The chief removed two tabloid newspapers and one magazine from a chair and sat down. "Her briefcase is gone too, so I guess she's hawking her novel."

Glenda finished with her customer at the cash register and cleaned around the chair. "Wayne, you should retire. I worry about you trying to keep peace in that cowtown out west. Robbers, murderers, kidnappers, cattle rustlers, you've been lucky so far. I think you ought to retire, get married—to Faye, maybe—and live a quiet, peaceful life. Do some traveling."

"I'd have to ease into it. So what's been happening in the Big Apple?"

"We're in the middle of a crime wave. A lot of people who've never had much money have been working in the war effort and now they've salted away sizable nest eggs. Con-men everywhere are trying their best to relieve the poor worker of his funds. They been talking about it on the radio. Why don't you turn it on? You might find it interesting."

"I might. You get the paper?"

"Faye took it. Usually they leave it on the front stoop, but I looked earlier and it's not there. You can get another at the newsstand on the corner."

In a few minutes, the chief held a cup of coffee and sat in a vacant hair-stylist's chair reading *The New York Times*. "Says here they're blaming the surge in crime on gangs of hoodlums terrorizing the neighborhoods."

"Naw, them boys just trying to get rid of their competition. They want to be the only ones doing anything illegal in their staked out area. So far they've been telling the store owners for a weekly fee they'll keep an eye out and not let anyone break the windows or steal the receipts. I give 'em ten dollars every Friday. It's cheap insurance."

"Glenda, turn on the radio. The mayor's going to make an announcement."

Glenda and Chief Wainwright listened for the next fifteen minutes to the mayor telling his listeners that if he's re-elected he's going to ask for more money so he can increase the number of cops walking their beats and revamp the police administration. Obviously, the mayor reasoned, the cop putting his life on the line is not getting the support he needs from his supervisors.

After the political speech a radio commentator gave his opinion.

"I got to get some fresh air. Those dimwits aren't going to reduce crime by simply beefing up the police force. They need to make some basic changes to the way they handle the perpetrators they catch. Make the punishment more in line with the offense. And if they would modernize their crime-scene procedures, they'd catch more of the bad guys to begin with."

Glenda reached for the telephone and dialed. In a few moments she said, "Yes, I'll hold." She handed the telephone to her brother, saying, "You should give your views to someone who can make use of them."

Chief Wainwright grabbed the phone and listened to see if he was actually on hold. In a moment a voice came through the telephone saying, "You're on the air. This morning we're talking about ways we can reduce crime. Have you got an opinion?"

"I sure do. I think the New York City Police Department needs to modernize. From reading the paper I've deciphered that less than half the crimes committed are solved. Then, those few times when the person accused is brought to trial, the authorities are so anxious to reduce crime that anyone tried is found guilty—whether guilty or not. Sometimes all they got is circumstantial evidence—or even hearsay. Then he's sentenced to a longer term than what the offense justifies. It's like beating little Mikey half to death for stealing unattended bread when someone else murdered Bob the baker."

"I see. And what is your name, sir?"

"Wainwright."

"Mr. Wainwright, do you have any experience fighting crime?"

"Yeah, I'm the chief of police in Dancing Deer, Arkansas."

23

"Stay on the line, Chief Wainwright. I'm going to take another call. Maybe we'll get an opinion of your assessment."

Glenda adjusted the radio dial and soon she and the chief could hear the broadcast. She cautioned the chief to stay a good distance from the radio with the telephone to keep the interference down.

"How the hell can a hick police officer from some podunk town in Arkansas think his crime-solving ability might be of any value to the people of New York City?"

"I don't know. This is Jerry, right?"

"Yeah."

"Let's take another caller. Hello, you're on *Crime-Watch Now*. You got an opinion on how to reduce crime?"

"No, I just want to tell that man from Arkansas that he better not be out after dark. He'll get mugged for sure. And, I want to know how many crimes he's solved this past year."

"Okay, I'll ask him." There was a slight pause and a few clicks. "Chief Wainwright. How big is Dancing Deer?"

"Somewhere between six and eight thousand."

"How many crimes have you solved this last year?"

"We don't have much crime in Dancing Deer. There's only been one homicide, a double, in the last four years and we have a state-wide manhunt for the suspect."

"Chief, is that all the experience you've got?"

"No, I've got thirty-five years in law enforcement. Just the last four in Dancing Deer."

"I see. Let me find out what our listeners have to say. Stay with me." Two minutes of commercials later. "Okay, we're back. Jerry, you got any comment?"

"I sure do. I've been to Arkansas. Every town in that state has a hanging tree. When someone commits a crime the men get together and decide who did it—bringing him to justice vigilante-style. They call themselves 'Baldknobbers.' Most of them towns don't even have a police force—just a Marshall toting a six-shooter."

"Now, Jerry, I don't think that's fair. Anyone else have an opinion?" Under his breath he said, "Man, all the lines are lighting up at the same time." There were a few clicks then, "You're on the air. We're talking about the increased crime in the city and we have Chief Wainwright from Dancing Deer, Arkansas, saying he knows how to put a stop to it. You got a comment?"

"Yes, sir. I can't believe the police departments in Arkansas are more modern that what we have in New York City. Ask him if he would elaborate."

"I'm sorry, but we're out of time. Call in tomorrow and we'll ask Chief Wainwright why his police department in Arkansas is so much better than the men in blue working for you."

The radio started talking about Flakey Crust Biscuits. From the telephone came, "Hey, Chief. That was pretty exciting. Can I get you to answer a few questions for our listeners tomorrow?"

"Sure. I'm not doing anything."

"Okay, give me your number and be by the telephone a few minutes before ten. You in town for a vacation? Business maybe?"

"Just taking a little time off and visiting my sister."

"I see. Then, you have family in the Big Apple?"

"Yeah. I was in administration for the New York City Police Department years ago, then got hired away by the people in Chicago. During the prohibition era I headed up their Organized Crime Task Force until I got in a power struggle with the FBI. I more or less retired after that to this sleepy little town in Arkansas."

"Uh, Chief. I think I'd rather have you come down to the radio station. You can sit here beside me and answer the listener's questions. Give me your address and I'll have a car pick you up. Is that all right with you, sir?"

"Yeah, sure."

CHAPTER 5 – FIRST GAME

"James Paul, when I shake my glove this way I'm going to throw a fast ball. No signal and it's going to be a curve. Sometimes I can make it drop sharply down and away at the last second. If I have that pitch working, I'll touch my belt. You give me a target over the center of the plate just above their kneecaps and I'll aim my pitches at your thumb or little finger, depending on whether they're crowding the plate or stepping in the bucket."

All James Paul could do was nod his head and tell Spider, "Yes, sir. Thank you, Mr. Spider."

Julius had taken over driving the bus from James Paul so his new catcher and Spider could go over their signals and then their responsibilities when backing up other players receiving balls thrown in from the outfield. Julius drove into the town of Martin and finding the high school parked under a shade tree fifty yards from the ball field. From branches Julius tied three quilts to erect a make-shift dressing room next to the bus.

Baby-Doll and her three helpers had arrived an hour earlier and had already set up the concession stand. The four women proceeded to make jerk-pork sandwiches. They also had spicy meat cooked inside pockets of dough. Baked golden brown and priced at a nickel each, these small but tasty morsels would be sold in multiples and handed over in paper sacks. The women carried them through the stands and sold them from boxes suspended by fabric straps circling behind their necks.

At the concession stand were pitchers of iced tea and galvanized buckets of iced beverages to go with the sandwiches. The third helper fixed the drinks and sold the sandwiches while Baby-Doll directed the entire operation and manned the till.

Julius made his players get dressed in their new red uniforms trimmed in black. For a half-dollar, a young boy made several trips lugging their equipment from the bus to the playing field.

27

"All right, listen up. Here's the starting lineup. We've already worked on the signals when batting and each of you knows how to play his position and what's expected. We want to play a clean game, keeping the score close until the last inning. Then we'll score enough runs to see us through any kind of rally they might muster and end up winning with you guys telling the other team how lucky we were and that they are a good bunch of players. We'll shake their hands and ease out of town with most of their spending cash. Any questions?"

"What if they're a really good team? Should we try and keep it close if they're as good as we?"

"No. If they're a good team I'll be able to tell during their warm-up and we'll play our best ball from the get. But we're not likely to find a team of that caliber. I'm sure we'll always be able to play good enough to win even when any other team's playing the best they're capable of. We just have to make the game enjoyable to the fans. Put on a show. Keep the fans happy and eating and drinking and forking over their money. Now, let's have some fun. Remember, don't talk back to the hecklers. There'll be hundreds of them and just a few of us. Everyone pair up and start limbering your arms. Spider, for about fifteen minutes throw soft. Don't throw anything hard until your arm has had plenty of time to warm up."

Back at the concession stand people were already lined up for drinks. Julius thought back to his first rule. Always start the game at meal-time. "Baby-Doll, you got your girls with the ticket-takers?"

"Yes. They know what to do. We'll get a good count of the attendance."

Besides keeping all the money made at the concessions, Julius split the admission receipts with the town. He also offered a thousand dollars to any team who could beat his New York Hotshots in a fairly contested nine innings of ball. Since just about every town had a baseball team, and the town had nothing to lose, he would make a pile of money—if his team won its games. Which they would. He'd spent quite a bit of effort working on their defense, then for the last few days he'd given instructions on hitting until he was hoarse, and his players took batting practice until they were begging for relief. They were ready. His only problem was that he didn't want to make it a laugher and get run out of town.

The stands filled up. Julius' boys sat along the first base side of the field, warmed up, and chomping at the bit. His opposition was on the field taking some grounders and lobbing the ball either to home or to first. Several slow rollers made it into the outfield. Julius casually observed their starting pitcher bringing on some heat to a coach with a catcher's mitt.

The opposing manager walked over with three men in tow. He held out his hand. "Name's Benson. These are the town's three ministers. The mayor said you only wanted the clergy officiating. We've got good umpires. Why not use them?"

Julius shook the extended hand. "Julius Mosivido. I'm not saying your umpires would not be fair, but we play about four games a week and, over the summer, we go to a lot of towns. If I don't make a requirement of that sort, then the law of averages will occasionally pit us against a pretty good team and a group of partial umpires. I can live with an umpire who misses a few strikes or tag-outs as long as he's doing his best to be fair. I think the town's ministers will be that kind of umpire. If they miss as many strikes for you as for me then that's all I can ask and you won't hear me complaining. I got a lot of money on the line. I just need to play on a level field."

Julius looked at the three ministers. He realized he had made a good choice in asking for their help and told them he had an extra face mask, strike clicker, and whisk for cleaning off home plate if the town didn't.

The youngest of the three ministers suggested the managers exchange scorecards and each give one to him. He slung a pouch containing three baseballs over his shoulder and walked behind the plate. With a loud bellow, similar to a call to worship, he shouted. "Play ball."

The fans cheered. The two young ladies with the dough pockets of spicy meat started going through the stands. At a nickel a piece, the dough pockets were selling fast. But as soon as the purchasing fans tasted them, they had to make a bee-line to the concession stand for something to drink.

In the top of the first, the Hotshots got the first two men on base with infield singles. They advanced on a passed ball and came home two outs later on a base-hit up the middle. The next man struck out.

In the bottom of the first, Spider struck out the first man and walked the second. The third man cracked a line drive between short and third. With runners now on the corners the batter hit a hard grounder to the second baseman. He tossed the ball underhanded to short, who stepped on the bag and threw a shot to first. It was the Hotshots' first double-play. There were lots of booing from the bleachers, but a lot of people from the bleachers were not in the bleachers. They were at the concession stand trying to get something to sooth scorched tongues. While the hot little dough pockets were almost given away, the beverages went for a premium.

By the fifth, the Hotshots were up seven to four and the concession stand had run out of drinks. Baby-Doll moved money from the till to her wardrobe several times, thinking people would get upset if it looked like the Hotshots were taking advantage of them with the cash box brimming full.

In the bottom of the seventh, Spider started getting tired. His pitches began to slowly inch up in the strike zone and one muscular young man hit the ball so hard no one could find it or pieces of it. The young man circled the bases and closed the gap separating the two teams to two.

In the top of the ninth, the Hotshots scored four runs and went into the bottom of the ninth leading eleven to five. In the bottom of the ninth, the local team scored three more before Spider struck out three successive batters. The Hotshots walked over to the opposing team and said they felt lucky. They said the locals were a fine team and the next time through it could just as easily be them on the winning side.

That night Julius pulled into Finks, the town for their second game, with eleven hundred and fifty-eight dollars from the concession sales and half the gate. They had a day off to drum up a nice crowd and to resupply the women with concession needs.

CHAPTER 6 – NEW YORK LISTENS

"Chief, I thought you were going to help me get my book published. Instead they've got you making appearances with the mayor. I can't even get in to see a publisher and the whole town wants you to become their new chief of police. You and I walk down the street and people we don't know walk up and ask for your autograph. Your picture has been in *The New York Times* three times this week and twice in *The Tribune*."

"Faye, I know. I've not been good to you. I'll make it up. I asked the producer of the radio program if he knew of somebody in the publishing industry. He said he'd take care of it. I'll have somebody look at your novel by this afternoon. I promise."

Tears ran down Faye's cheeks. She put her arms around the chief's neck and kissed him. "Oh, W.W., that's wonderful."

"Now, Doll, listen, I've got to go to city hall with the mayor this morning. He wants to give me a tour of the downtown police headquarters and then he wants me to stand behind him at his press conference this afternoon. You stay close to the telephone. A man by the name of Dandy Randy will call to give you an address and an appointment time. Here's my limo. I've got to go. Faye, it's your big chance. Go knock 'em dead, Doll, and I'll take you to this great Italian restaurant for a celebration meal tonight."

At three o'clock that afternoon, Faye Spencer opened the door to the sumptuous offices of the Crito, Crito, and Steadman Publishing House. She took a seat while the receptionist rang Maxine Crito.

In a few minutes another woman entered the reception area and walked up to Faye. "Miss Spencer, will you follow me?"

Inside Maxine Crito's office, Faye was seated and then had to wait for Maxine to finish looking through a short stack of papers. "Miss Spencer, I thought a Mr. Wainwright was the one asking for an appointment."

"No. He's a friend who's promised to help me get published."

"I see. This Mr. Wainwright does seem to have the proper connections." Maxine looked at Faye. "Have you ever written anything before?"

"I've been an investigative reporter for several newspapers in Arkansas. This story is about a double murder that took place in our town. Actually, the first on the floor beneath my apartment and the second outside my apartment window. During the trial of the suspected murderer, I was kidnapped and held for ransom by, I believe, the actual murderer. I wrote the story while his captive and then escaped."

"Is this Mr. Wainwright the Arkansas detective currently making the rounds with our mayor?"

"Yes."

"Did he help you write it?"

"No. The story is entirely mine."

"I see. Do you think Mr. Wainwright might be interested in writing a forward, giving an endorsement, or make some comment we could use on the dust jacket?"

"I don't know. I really think he wants this case behind him."

"Miss Spencer, here's what I can do. If you were represented by an agent and had Mr. Wainwright write something we could include, I would certainly give it some thought."

"Mrs. Crito, this is my book. Mr. Wainwright's a friend. I'm sure he'd do anything I asked, but I don't want to ask. The book is good enough on its own. If you would just read it you'd see that we could easily forego the formalities and go straight to a publishing contract."

"Unfortunately, Miss Spencer, that's not the way we do business. Think it over and give me a call. You can leave word with my secretary." At this Maxine pushed a button on her desk and her personal assistant promptly entered the room.

"Betty, will you see Miss Spencer out?"

Faye wanted to say something, but Maxine had already picked up a group of papers and started shuffling through.

That night Faye waited for Chief Wainwright. She was in a foul mood. So far this trip had not gone as she'd planned. She wanted to be in the spotlight, not off to one side while W.W. walked center stage. She didn't even want to share the spotlight with him. This trip was for her.

At dinner, W.W. wore a new white dinner jacket and black satin bowtie. He looked like he belonged in the spotlight. Faye had on the same dress she'd put on that morning. It was still fairly clean with only a few wrinkles, but it certainly wasn't a gown. She wondered what people thought when they looked her way.

"Faye, have you heard that they've caught Sheriff Shodtoe? Jellico is defending him. So far no one has found the Bonds boy. His dad came into town and picked up the Plymouth. Jellico says his preparation for the trial's not going well. Pepe and Harriet are somewhere out west, and Jellico says he did such a good job painting Shodtoe as the villain that he's having the dickens of a time with public opinion. No one wants to believe there might be someone else involved. He called this afternoon asking if there was anything we could remember that he might've missed. What do you think? What happened to that Bonds kid anyway?"

"I don't know. He told me not to come out of my room. Several times he came in and handcuffed me to a radiator. He said he didn't have a key and couldn't have me just walking out."

"But that's what you did."

"What?"

"Walked out."

"Yes. I ran out of food. All he gave me to eat was a sack of sardines and Vienna sausages and a few cans of potted meat. I finally finished my book and couldn't stomach another smelly fish so I went looking for him. If I'd found him, I'd have torn him apart. A hungry woman who hasn't had a bath in a week is not someone to mess with."

"So when you didn't find him you left?"

"Yeah. I looked the place over, turned on lights where I could, and looked in all the rooms. When I decided he wasn't there, I went to the back door and turned the lock. After not seeing light for two weeks, I was blinded when the door opened."

Chief Wainwright had a perplexed look on his face. He then reached over and put his hand on hers. Slowly he said, "Faye, what was it Bill told us about his efforts to sell the building?"

"He said he brought in a prospective buyer. That he'd spent all his liquid assets and, with the bank examiners looking over his books, he couldn't take out enough money for my ransom."

"No. What did he and this prospective buyer find?"

"Nothing. Bill said he lowered the price to fifteen thousand less than what he'd paid a few days earlier, but the buyer said it was too dark. Then they heard a loud click and the buyer thought the building had rats. He said he didn't want it at any price."

"That's what I remembered him saying." The chief took a drink of Pinot Grigio and with a solemn look said, "Faye, this is your chance. This is what you've been waiting for. You can solve this case. You know where that Bonds boy is. Just put the pieces of the puzzle together."

"What are you talking about?"

The waiter walked up with their entrées. He refilled their wine glasses and set down slices of bread covered with butter and garlic then smothered in cheese and toasted. In another dish he poured flakes of red pepper and ground up white peppercorns. He splashed on extra-virgin olive oil. Over their entrée he grated bits of mozzarella cheese. "Is there anything else I can get for you?"

Neither Chief Wainwright nor Faye Spencer answered. The chief looked into the dazzling green eyes of Faye Spencer and Faye Spencer looked back in her memory at the events as they had unfolded.

After a few more minutes of silence, Faye smiled. She whispered, "I do know where he is."

CHAPTER 7 – THE STINK

"Men, our town's been challenged to a ball game by Skunk Hollow. I've called this City Council Meeting to address two issues. Number one—should we play them? And, number two—how can we make any money out of it?

"Mr. Nelson, you've got your hand raised. Would you care to address either of these issues?"

"Yes, sir, Mayor Bob. I think it's a matter of civic pride. We got to play them—unless we can come up with a reasonable excuse not to. And, if we do play them, we got to win. A loss to Skunk Hollow and I'd have to leave town. Does anyone know if they're any good?"

"I heard they took quite a thrashing from that Negro League team travelling through. Didn't get a hit in all nine innings off some pitcher named Satchel. Of course that negro team whupped every team they played. They got such a reputation that, eventually, none of the towns they came to would field a team for fear of embarrassment. They had to start choosing up sides and playing games among themselves. I heard the men from Skunk Hollow went on to play some other towns in south Arkansas, losing a few and winning a few."

"Yeah, but look at the experience they got. We don't even have a team. When do they want to play?"

Mayor Bob grabbed his letter and silently read through. In a moment he came to the sentence he was looking for. "July the fourth."

"Well, I think we ought to play 'em if we played 'em here. We could sell tickets and slices of watermelon. Make a fortune. We could even hype up our team, let everybody think they're the best anywhere. Then, place a few discreet wagers on Skunk Hollow to win."

Jerry mumbled, "I'd have to visit my family in Branson for a few weeks."

Mayor Bob said, "Okay, then we're agreed we'll play them if the game is held here and we get to keep the gate receipts. I'll let them

35

think we'll play them next on their field and they'll keep the admission ticket sales and concessions for that game."

Bill Potter raised his hand. "Gentlemen, we can't go into this expecting to lose. What's more, we don't have uniforms, equipment, or even a decent place to play."

Amid the increased level of rumbling, Mayor Bob raised both hands, palms down. "I think our team needs a sponsor. Someone who'll buy the uniforms to have his name embroidered on the back. Bill, would your bank be interested?"

"I dunno. I think I'd rather have my bank's name on the backs of the Skunk Hollow men."

Someone down the line said, "What we gonna name our team? What name does the Skunk Hollow men go by?"

"I think they're called the 'Skunk Hollow Stink.'"

"You've got to be kidding."

"He is. They're the 'Skunk Hollow Polecats.'"

"Sounds redundant to me."

"So how about calling our men the 'Dancing Deer Soft-Shoe?'"

"They're going to get their butts kicked. I say we call them the 'Dancing Deer Peckerwoods.'"

Bill Potter stood up and waited for the laughter to subside. "Okay, that's it. I'll finance the team. I'll buy the uniforms and all the equipment. I'll even find a place to play and have a backstop erected." He paused a moment then said, "Any of you squirrels brave enough to field a position?" He looked around the room. "I didn't think so. I'll give even odds to anyone wanting to make a side wager that our guests will win. Any amount you can scrape together." Bill grabbed his briefcase. "I think we'll let the town name the team. Gentlemen, this meeting is over."

CHAPTER 8 – SHODTOE'S PRE-TRIAL

Jellico opened his briefcase and pulled out a stack of papers. "Sherman, do any of these prospective jurors have anything against you?"

"Let's see." Sheriff Shodtoe shuffled through the sheets. "I've served papers on a few. This man spent a few nights in the county jail for beating his wife. I had to release him when she wouldn't press charges. She had a black eye and was missing a front tooth but said she couldn't live without her man. And this guy got busted for cock-fighting."

"I see. Well, it looks like I'll have to do a records check on each. Are there any friends or relatives mixed in?"

"Yeah. Caroline is the wife of a cousin and this woman was a dispatcher for a while. You better cross her off. I don't think she left on the best of terms. And Aaron was a high-school friend. We were best buds until his parents decided he needed to travel in different circles. I don't recognize the rest. You should have pictures to go with the names."

"That's a good idea. If I have many more murder trials I'll include that service and jack up my fee."

"You found the Bonds boy yet?"

"No. He vanished. His dad swears he hasn't seen him and the kid hasn't contacted his brother at the Tucker Farm. I have to keep looking. Without him our case stinks to high heaven."

"You shouldn't have done such a good job getting Bill Potter off. Now, everybody in town is absolutely certain I'm the killer and this Bonds boy is really a figment of my imagination; he's someone I made up to cover my ass."

"I charged Potter ten times what I'm charging you. For him I had three people gathering information—one of them a seasoned private-eye from France. But they're all gone. I'm having to work your case by myself."

"Hey, have they charged Raymond with anything?" asked the sheriff.

"No. Emmett thought about charging him with aiding and abetting a fugitive and tampering with evidence, but cut him a deal instead. He's now their star witness. In return for his testimony he's not being charged with anything. What'll he be testifying about, Sherman?"

"I don't know. He never saw the Bonds boy. But I did talk him into planting that gun in Bill's car. And I gave him five hundred dollars of my contract money for killing Hamelin."

"Your trial's turning out to be more difficult than Bill's. Everyone's so damn sure you did it and this ball game is a scant two weeks away. No one's paying you much mind. They think you'll be convicted and fried before winter. I doubt we'll have a full house unless I can generate some excitement. Say, Sherman, what was the telescope for?"

"Surveillance."

"Why was it on a tripod and pointed at Faye Spencer's bedroom window?"

"I was just making sure she was safe. You think they'll let me out to see the ballgame?"

Jellico went to Faye Spencer's apartment to see her sister Katy. He needed help and Katy had shown an aptitude for solving crimes when she once slid through the cracks to join his team. He knocked on her door.

"Hello, Mr. Jellico. Come in. I'd planned on calling you. How's Sherman's trial coming along?"

"Not so good, Katy. Emmett has a solid case. And now he's getting Raymond to testify that Sheriff Shodtoe told him and his two deputies to find your husband. I don't think Sherman killed Galen, but he'd planned on doing it."

"Would you like something to drink, Mr. Jellico?"

"No. Thank you, Katy. But would you please start calling me Jellico? If my father were still around you could call him Mr. Jellico." Jellico eased onto an empty loveseat. "Have you heard from your sister?"

"Yes, I have. She sent a telegram saying she and Chief Wainwright would be back in time for the trial."

"Anything else?"

"No, but you know how those telegrams work. They charge by the word."

"Katy, would you have some spare time to chase down leads for me? Sherman doesn't have a lot of money, but I think he can afford to pay for a detective. And you're plenty smart. I think we would make a good team. What do you say?"

"I think that would be fantastic. Where do you want me to start?"

"I think one of the Johnson deputies pulled over Evan Bonds just up the highway from where he run Pepe off the road. We'll need a copy of his ticket and you can interview Rafe or Ralph to see if they noticed anything unusual. Then Daniel Poul has been released. We need to get him a subpoena before he leaves town. Do you think Gleason Bonds will testify that he sent his younger brother to steal Daniel's money from Raylene?"

"No. That might keep him from getting a parole."

"Yeah. That's what I thought. But a woman with an ability to twist men up like pretzels might be able to convince him it would be in his best interest."

"That's asking a lot, Jellico."

"You're right. Why don't you come by my office tomorrow and we'll discuss what Emmett sent over in the discovery process. I also have his list of witnesses."

CHAPTER 9 – RECRUITING

"Jesse, I need you to run an article on the town of Dancing Deer being challenged to a baseball game by the Polecats from Skunk Hollow."

"Mr. Potter, have a seat. We've already sent a reporter to Skunk Hollow to check out the challenge. And we got another reporter in Russellville watching the Polecats play the Russellville Hayseeds."

Bill Potter was walking in circles, wringing his hands. "I think I've made a bad decision. We can't beat Skunk Hollow. They've got a seasoned team with a dozen games under their belts. I'm seriously considering canceling the game to avoid the embarrassment."

"What can I do to help?" Jesse Bell offered the town banker a cup of coffee.

"Do you know of someone with a blazing fastball?"

"Yep."

"You do?"

"Yep."

Bill Potter took the coffee cup, added cream, and drank it down. "Okay, who is it?"

"Jedidiah Calhoun. In David Blaine's room, I've seen pictures of his dad in his heyday. David said his dad once struck out seventeen batters in a seven-inning game. I guess they play seven innings in high school."

"Hell, yes. I remember that game. He wore out two catchers. One batter asked the umpire if he was sure the pitch that struck him out was over the plate, saying he'd blinked. The umpire said he thought so, but couldn't be sure with his eyes closed. But, that was in 1918. Jed's now over forty. You think he can still bring it?"

"Yep."

"Okay. I got to go talk to him. You know any more good players?"

41

"Yeah, Paul Nelson, Wally Braxton, and your son-in-law. I'll run an article in the paper asking for anyone wanting to participate in the humiliation of the Skunk Hollow Polecats to show up at the high school ball field with their gloves and bats. Who's gonna be the manager?"

"I thought I might, or do you have somebody else in mind?"

"Old man Ridley played professional for Pittsburg before the turn of the century. I'll bet he'd make a good manager or at least be able to help you pick the right players."

"You know, Jesse, I'm glad I came to see you. I'm feeling better already."

Bill's next stop was the high-school ball field. It looked more like a pasture than a place to play ball. To himself Bill said, "Won't be many homeruns with no outfield fence. I got to get someone to mow. I also have to order equipment. Maybe I'll head over to old man Ridley's. He's too old to play, but he might be able to help me get the ones we come up with into shape."

Later that afternoon, Bill called a sporting goods store in Little Rock. He ordered three bases and their pegs, a dozen gloves, two dozen assorted Louisville Slugger baseball bats, an umpire's mask, and all the catcher's equipment. He decided to hold off on the uniforms until he knew the sizes. He then called Jed Calhoun.

"Jed, you'll never guess our good fortune. The Polecats from Skunk Hollow have challenged us to a game of baseball. The town gets to charge admission and keep all of the receipts as well as any food and beverages we might sell."

"And you're putting this together?"

"Damn straight. At the city council meeting I more or less said I'd take charge. They were of the mind that we'd be humiliated and didn't want any part in it, until they thought there might be some money to be made. Then they thought they'd man the turn-stiles and sell concessions with sacks over their heads. Say, Jed, do you know anybody who knows how to play ball?"

"Just a few old-timers. Baseball is now a young man's sport. Too much running—you got to be lightning fast to make it to the big leagues."

"How about David Blaine? Didn't he play in high school?"

"No. He worked every summer. He knows how to play though—just never got much chance. Still, he might be a good candidate. He and I used to play catch every afternoon before we were called to supper."

"How about you, Jed. You're still lean and agile. Not like some of us. Me for instance. I've gone to seed. I now huff and puff just running to my car when it rains. You want to be the starting pitcher?"

"No. You'd be better off letting some young stallion pull your cart."

"Now, Jed, I can't believe you'd let an opportunity to show Emily what a stud you once were slide by without giving it a shot. I remember watching you pitch in high school. You threw hard and a little wild. The batters on the other team stood at the plate with their knees shaking. They couldn't force themselves to stand close enough to hit anything—even if they had the nerve to swing. We always had the sorriest defense because they seldom got an opportunity to field a ball."

"Bill, that's only about half true."

"How about helping me coach then? You can play a few innings, take yourself out at any time, and then be the coach at first. I'll coach at third. We'll set the starting lineup and who's going to play where, together. How about it, 'Easy.' That's what they called you wasn't it—'Easy Money' Calhoun. You were cash in hand."

"Yeah. When you going to have your prospects show up?"

"This weekend at the high school ball field."

"Okay, I'll be there."

The next day most of the members of the city council came by Bill's bank. When Bill arrived at nine Mayor Bob was sitting in the reception area waiting.

"Good morning, Robert. You finally going to open an account?"

"No. I want to take advantage of your offer. Here's seven hundred dollars. You said you'd give even money to any of us who think Skunk Hollow will win. My money says you can't get a team together in three weeks that can beat 'em. You want me to give my stakes to your secretary?"

"No, that won't be necessary. Just sign a slip saying how much you're wagering." Bill turned to his secretary. "Carla, make sure the paper lists the terms of the wager. He's picking Skunk Hollow to beat Dancing Deer in a game of baseball on July fourth of this year for even money." Bill turned back. "Bob, you got an old Ford tractor I'll let you put up for another four hundred."

"It's a deal."

Carla wrote out two sheets of paper and Mayor Bob signed both. Another member of the city council entered as he was leaving. Bill told Carla she better write out several sheets of paper and then she could simply fill in the blanks. It looked like most of the city council would be coming by for the soft money he was giving away.

It was Wednesday and the paper was read in the homes, work-shops, beauty parlors, retail stores, barns, and park benches. Jesse had written a stirring call-to-arms and everyone wanted to be a part of the ass-kicking they would be handing to the upstarts from down the road. Soon it was the main topic of conversation and several telephone calls tried to locate Bill and secure a position on the team. When Bill was accosted on the sidewalks, in the bank, or sitting at his regular table at the Ritz Hotel Bistro, he had to say the positions were all up for grabs and tryouts were at the high-school ball field Saturday morning.

CHAPTER 10 – TRYOUTS

Jesse and his photographer were there to document the events. Women sat in the bleachers and under the trees, with some handing out mason jars of water and iced tea. Kids played under the bleachers and around the trees, some chased errant balls. The men paired off to play catch and limber up their arms, so when they did get to throw something with a little zip it would leave a little zip in the arm.

Carla got everyone's name and the position he thought he was best suited to play. Most brought their own gloves. One man wearing overalls was catching with a glove he had for shoveling coal and building fences. There were even some make-shift bats turned at the Moccasin Gap sawmill.

Bill let out a big sigh of relief when the Calhouns arrived. He saw Jed and Emily, two of Jed's three daughters, his daughter, Rose, and her husband, David Blaine. Rose also brought his grandson, Little Carson.

As soon as Little Carson got out of the car he spied his grandpa and ran at breakneck speed, hitting and almost knocking Bill to the ground. Bill was observing someone with better than average skills with the glove and staggered a few feet from the collision.

"Whoa, little fella. You gonna be a football player? You got a glove? Stay close to your papaw. There's loose balls flying everywhere."

Someone walked up from behind and lightly touched Bill's shoulder. "Can you use someone a little long in the tooth?"

"Mr. Ridley. How are you, sir?"

"I'm still kicking."

"I had planned on talking to you about helping to manage the team. But I see you've brought a bat and glove . . . uh, sir, do you want to play?"

"Wherever I can be of most benefit."

"What's with the bat? It looks like a broom stick—longer and skinnier than most."

"Son, this here's a fungo bat. If you want to see if anyone can catch a decent fly ball I'll use it to knock a few to the outfield."

Bill turned to the players. "You six head to the outfield. You six take positions between second and third. Paul, you play first. Jed hit them some ground balls and have them throw to first. Make note of the ones with a strong arm. Maybe Rose will write down your observations. Let David catch. Me and Mr. Ridley are going to see if anyone can catch a fly ball. In an hour we'll switch players."

Bill handed Jed a bat and a sack of baseballs. He then headed down the first base line with another sack of balls, a glove, and Mr. Ridley.

Mr. Ridley boomed out, "You fellers are too close. Most of these balls are gonna go over your heads."

Four moved back. Two stayed close, mumbling to themselves how a man ninety years old couldn't hit a ball over their heads. Mr. Ridley took one of the balls from the sack, tossed it into the air, and knocked it high over the heads of the two players standing close. The ball also went over the heads of the ones who had moved back.

Mr. Ridley reached into the sack held out by a stunned Bill Potter. "Damn, that felt good."

For the next thirty minutes, Mr. Ridley belted one long ball after another. The men were wheezing when Bill yelled it was time for a water break. On the infield, Paul Nelson had given way to someone else at first. He sat on a bench, two men sat on the edge of the outfield grass, three players still fielded balls, and four had went home.

After a short break, Bill traded men with Jed and hit balls to the outfield while Mr. Ridley observed the abilities of the men shagging the fly balls heading their way.

After a second water break, Bill picked one man to take batting practice. Half of the remainder got into the outfield and everyone else was sprinkled around the infield. Jed lobbed balls over the plate while David Blaine caught. When the batter had swung at about ten to fifteen pitches he headed to the outfield, one of the outfielders came to the infield, and one of the infielders headed to the plate.

Bill gave his team an appraising look. Jed lobbed 'em up easy and most of the men were swinging out of their britches. Sometimes a batter would get a hit, but more often they were cork-screwing holes in the batter's box. Twisting around like an augur, they were trying to hit a ball like the Babe or maybe Stan the Man would. In the outfield everyone was sitting down. On the infield only two men stood. To Bill, it looked like he had a lazy team.

After the last man batted, Bill said he'd like to take a turn. He picked up a likely piece of lumber, took a few waggles, and told Jed to let her rip. Jed put a little more on the ball and Bill hit a hard grounder to short.

"Damn, Jed, is that all you got?"

The next one come in high and tight—and hard. Bill bailed, landing on his butt.

"Now that's more like it. Put one of those puppies over the plate."

The next pitch was down the center, but Bill was late getting around and, even though he had a mighty cut, he just swished vacant air.

"Okay, that's good enough for me. Men, we'll be practicing every afternoon after work. If you can't make a practice, try and make the next one so you can keep your spot on the team. See ya'll Monday afternoon."

CHAPTER 11 – CAMPAIGNING

"Faye, take this hundred and buy yourself a new dress. We're invited to a gala at the Waldorf Astoria. The Mayor wants us to sit at his table. I've had him invite Maxine Crito as well. She'll be sitting directly across from you. I'm trying my best, Doll, to make good on my promise."

"Oh, W.W., you should have given me a warning. I need time to think of what to say."

"I'm sorry, but we just got the notice this morning. I thought I was pretty fast on the draw asking for Mrs. Crito to be included. The mayor thinks it's going to be a hoot."

"What are we celebrating?"

"Nothing in particular. It's a fundraiser, allowing each person the opportunity to slip five hundred dollars into the mayor's campaign war chest."

"Chief, can you afford such an expensive evening?"

"Oh, sure. The radio station's paying my contribution. They even gave me that hundred as spending money. We'll talk about the evening tomorrow on the broadcast. Have you heard I've been asked to appear on television right after today's noon local news?"

"No, I haven't. How's that going to differ from your radio interviews?"

"Pretty much the same except my appearance will be under scrutiny. And there will be a different audience "

"Are you going to take the job of chief of police if the mayor's re-elected and offers it?"

"Probably not. I'm enjoying the notoriety, but really don't want to get into the nitty-gritty. Besides, our plan was to get you a publisher and head home to a hero's welcome. I'm not planning on wavering from my agreement. You'll find I'm pretty much a straight shooter."

"I'm learning things about you all the time, W.W."

"Today we have with us W.W. Wainwright. He's the chief of police in Dancing Deer, Arkansas, and has some interesting commentary on how to combat the increasing crime in our city. The mayor has latched onto him and now, when you see the mayor, you see Chief Wainwright in the background.

"On the panel to ask Chief Wainwright questions we have our station manager, Bob Boyd Brown, and two newspaper columnists: Jim Strickland from *The Times* and Janie Bowman from *The Tribune*. But before we start with their barrage, I have some questions of my own I'd like to ask W.W. Is it all right if I call you W.W?"

"It depends. If you're going to ask me questions I can't answer—or won't answer—then we should probably keep things formal. However, if you're genuinely interested in my opinions then you can call me whatever you want."

"I see. How about we start off on middle ground by letting me call you Chief?"

"Fair enough."

"Okay, Chief. Why the upsurge in crime?"

"I don't think there has been an increase in violent crime. Murders, rapes, and armed robbery are at the same per capita rate as before the war. But what has increased are the lesser crimes of purse snatching, robbery, arson, vandalism, and con schemes. Also, white collar crime is up. We have more stealing of intellectual property, embezzlement, unfair trade practices, price gouging, and employees not getting fair treatment from their employers."

"So, Chief, why is this?"

"I think, with the men off to war and the women taking their places in the workforce, there's little supervision at home for our youth. The people providing guidance, the ability to decide what's right from what's wrong, and who to associate with are wearing too many hats.

"Churches have stepped up with youth centers and organized activities, as well as organizations such as the Y.M.C.A. But what we have to do is recognize the problem and start to address the underlying cause before it gets completely out of hand."

"I think I now understand the increase in purse snatching and vandalism, but what about the con schemes?"

"Well, with low unemployment and our industry booming, the good people of this great city have more dinero than ever. Some of these citizens, now with discretionary funds, are not using good discretion when deciding how to spend their coin. If an opportunity comes along that sounds too good to be true, it probably is. John Q Public needs to salt some of his, or her, money away instead of investing in get-rich-quick schemes."

"And the white collar crime?"

"We're at war. The watchdogs are busy. More money is at stake than ever before. These are the only enticements some people need to pilfer from the corporate pocketbook. And while the media focuses on violent crimes, boring white-collar crime goes unnoticed. Sometimes it does get second-page billing, but certainly not front-page like a homicide."

"Okay, New York. This is what a man from Arkansas thinks about our burgeoning problem of crime. What's your opinion? Chief Wainwright is a regular on Dandy Randy's morning broadcast titled *Crime-Watch Now* on radio station WUPR. We'll be back to listen to the Chief field questions from our experts after these important announcements from our sponsors."

Chief Wainwright shifted his weight. Would he be able to answer the questions? Would he be at a loss for words? Would he stammer or cough—or worse—burp into the microphone? Was this what life in the circus would have been like?

When the show resumed the chief was not prepared for Miss Bowman's first question. "Mr. Wainwright, are you married?"

For the next half-hour Chief Wainwright parried with three intelligent questioners. He answered their questions, interjected bits of commentary on famous cases he had been involved with, and gave everyone a brief glimpse into the everyday life of a modern crime-fighter. When the program was over, the people on his questioning panel and the station's viewers held a high regard for their out-of-state visitor.

CHAPTER 12 – THE PRE-GAME

"Men, we have a definite problem. Bill has put together a team that could possibly win. I still think it's unlikely, but what if he pulls the upset? I mean . . . I've bet every penny I could scrape together and even put up my tractor. If Dancing Deer wins I'll be eating hard-tack for a year."

Jerry Millhouse said, "Mayor Bob, we're all in the same boat. I took out a loan for the money I bet."

Harold Greenleaf squirmed in his chair. "I didn't borrow any money, but if we lose I'm gonna be mighty pissed-off. Does anyone have an opinion as to how we can guarantee the Peckerwoods will lose?"

"Has anyone been able to determine what Nelson's planning on doing? I understand he had Roger bet five hundred for him before Bill asked him to play first. Now he's gotta make up his mind how important that money is."

"I talked to him. He's in a stew. He wants to play well, he wants Dancing Deer to win, and he wants to win his wager."

"Let's forget about him. He's a pig in a poke. What else can we do?"

Mayor Bob said, "I may have solved our problem. My uncle is one of the umpires and I told him it'd be worth a hundred dollars if Skunk Hollow wins. That's ten apiece."

Jerry Millhouse jumped up from his chair. "I say we chip in thirty apiece, call him up, and say it's worth three hundred. I'd sleep a lot easier."

"Yeah. I second it."

"Thirty seems fair to me."

Harold Greenleaf said, "Gentlemen, I think we really don't have much to worry about. Skunk Hollow has been playing all summer. They have a winning record with losses only to that troupe of barnstormers from the Negro League, the Russellville Hayseeds, the Clarksville

Wolverines, and Scranton's Screeching Owls. I think they've won six or more games and came close in all but one of their losses. I vote against bribing an umpire. Besides, if he calls the bases, he won't have that much impact anyway."

"He's the one calling balls and strikes."

"In that case, thirty dollars might be a prudent investment. Is Bill taking any more bets?"

"Haven't heard, but I stole two hundred dollars from my wife's egg money. She's been saving two years to buy a new quilting machine. I thought I'd get with Bill as soon as our meeting's over."

Mayor Bob stood up. "Okay, lets take a vote. All those in favor of offering my uncle three hundred to make sure Skunk Hollow wins raise your hands." Hands shot up all around the room. "Well then, that's that. It's unanimous. This meeting is adjourned. There's traps to be laid and wagers to be made."

On July fourth, at ten-thirty in the morning, Pepe Martel pulled into town driving an eight cylinder 1933 Duesenberg, Model J. Pepe drove sitting on three folded towels he swiped from a famous hotel in Malibu. Bedore the towels he'd had a difficult time seeing the road from the business side of a massive mahogany steering wheel. The Duesenberg was a big car normally driven by big men. Pepe was a big man—everywhere except in stature. He had big ideas, big plans, big endeavors, and big performances. He thought of himself as a big man. His children thought he was a big man. The women in his life thought he was a big man. Somehow fate thought otherwise and saddled him with a slight build, maybe to see how he would react. He reacted by doing everything in a big way.

At sixty-five, Pepe was closing in on old age and finally convinced himself he needed to slow down. But first he'd brought his daughter from France, following her dream. She met Jesse Bell, the proprietor of the small-town newspaper and fell in love. After a couple of months of wedded bliss she informed her father she was pregnant. Pepe then whisked Bill Potter's ex-wife off to see the sights of the Western United States before coming back to check on his daughter. He'd planned on then heading back to France to rebuild his winery from being shutdown for the duration of the war.

54

Harriet received a telegram while Pepe was scuba diving in the Sea of Cortez. It said the town of Dancing Deer was to play a game of baseball against another town. There was a rumor going around that Bill Potter had bet his bank that Dancing Deer would win even though they had never played a game. The other team was heavily favored by anyone with the least bit of baseball knowledge. Harriet asked Pepe to bring her back in time for the game even though he'd planned on staying in the United States and sightseeing the west until it was time for the baby to be born sometime in December or January—still months away.

So, after two months and change, Pepe drove back to Dancing Deer. When the game and a little socializing had been performed, he and Harriet would continue their American journey by heading to Florida to see the Everglades and to hunt the American alligator.

Pepe pulled the big car into the parking garage of the Ritz Grand Hotel and Ballroom. It wouldn't fit in a normal parking space so he parked at an angle, taking up two spaces.

"Harriet, I should never have let you talk me into buying such a big damn car."

"Oh, like I could have talked you out of it. When you saw the 'Duesy' you were so nervous, thinking the man wouldn't sell, that you kept offering more money. And that's after he'd agreed to a price. It's only because he didn't understand French that we had enough money left to eat on. It took almost a week for your bank to wire more funds."

"Well, it's mine now and, after our whirlwind tour of the states, I'm going to ship it home."

"Pepe, you check us in. Remember, two rooms like we discussed. I'm going to call Willie and see what's going on."

"Mon Cherie, he's got to know . . . I mean we've been gone for almost three months and I sure as hell didn't need a secretary."

"Pepe! You promised."

"Yes, I did. And I'll keep the promise. You have the word of a gentleman on that."

Harriet unwrapped her headscarf, straightened her clothes, and, grabbing her purse, headed to a telephone.

"Willie, it's so good to hear your voice. Tell me about this ball game. Sure . . . I'm down in the lobby. Say, fifteen minutes? Okay, see you then."

Pepe approached and handed her the key to her room. It was on the third floor. Even though he and Harriet had had a wonderful time, he'd decided to go back to France and see if the lady he left in Vichy was still waiting. She was the woman he saw when he closed his eyes, the woman he heard in the shower. She was the woman he dreamed about. He thought about her wearing his shirt over supple skin. The way her hair bounced when she walked. Harriet was a wonderful woman, but Odette was the love of his life.

Pepe called his daughter.

"Oh, Papa, I'm so glad you're back. Did you come for the game? David's playing. I've been sitting in the bleachers watching him practice for the last week. He's so good. Papa, you're going to love this game of baseball. Shall I pick you up? It starts at one, but Jesse is already there. I've packed roast beef sandwiches—I'll put in more for you. We can get beverages there, but nothing alcoholic. They have weird laws about when and where you can drink."

"Genevieve, are you feeling okay? I mean the baby's still . . ."

"Yes, Papa, me and the baby are just fine. I'll be right there. You have to tell me about your trip west."

"Dad, you feeling all right?"

"Yeah, just worried. Three weeks wasn't enough time to prepare. No one seems to know what to do. There's a lot of enthusiasm and team spirit, but we lack the fundamentals. We haven't had enough people to play scrimmage games and our offense is anemic. We have a few good defensive players. Daniel Poul is a good shortstop and Paul Nelson plays a good first, but Bear doesn't have much range in center and, although Leonard has a strong arm at third, he's wild, pulling Paul off first about half the time to catch the ball. And, no one knows how to field a bunt. Son, I think we're in for a long day."

"I've heard several men have placed heavy wagers on us losing."

"Probably safe bets."

"It may be, but, Dad, I hate like the dickens to lose."

"You and me too. We'll go out there and do our best. Maybe it'll be good enough. Go tell the women it's time to go."

When the Calhouns arrived, coaches, umpires, players, and a few early fans milled around and admired how nice the field looked.

Early on, a farmer brought in a herd of sheep. He divided the field down the middle and let his sheep graze on half while water sprinklers watered the other half. The next day he switched, only taking them off long enough for the team to get in its practice. Another farmer added a few goats, saying the sheep would do a good job on the grass, but his goats were needed for the weeds. Over the short period before the game, the field changed into one any sand-lot player would be proud to call home.

The day before the game, a team of workers wearing olive green shirts with The First Bank and Trust of Dancing Deer embroidered on the back, removed the animals, raked and carted off their refuse, sprinkled sand over the outfield, and rolled the entire field with a drum full of water. They also raked and cleaned the infield of any rocks and hard clogs of dirt.

The morning of the game, the workers did a final raking of the infield before laying string to guide their sprinkling lines of lime for the base paths and batter's boxes on both sides of home plate. When the buses from Skunk Hollow arrived everything was set.

"Willie, you never did like playing baseball. You must've played every sport we had but not baseball. Why now?"

"Because the members of the city council made fun of the town's ability to answer the challenge. One of them even said we should name the team the Dancing Deer Peckerwoods, because we were going to get our butts kicked."

"Ha, ha. Peckerwoods. That's funny. But what is the relationship between the term 'Peckerwoods' and getting your butts kicked?"

"I don't know, but it infuriated me just the same and I made it a cause célèbre. And the town responded. We might not win this game, but when it's over those Polecats from Skunk Hollow will know they were in a game."

"Willie, I should have been here. I was a regular member of the Royal Rooters; sat next to 'Nuff Said' McGreevy himself. I attended almost every home game they played, but you know that already. Is there anything I can do?"

"You might sit in the play-by-play booth. Jesse will be announcing the batters as they come up, but he might need help keeping the line-up straight and the strike count correct."

"No problem. Willie, you sure look handsome in that ball uniform. Can I walk you to the ball field?"

"Sure. The catering truck has already delivered the gear and all the food for the concessions. The men from the city council are taking turns manning the gate and the concession stand. The city stands to make several hundred dollars." Bill carefully positioned his royal blue baseball cap. "I'm ready if you are."

CHAPTER 13 – THE POLECATS

Bill walked to the manager of the Skunk Hollow team and held out his hand. The Skunk Hollow manager slapped it instead and grinned. He had very little respect for a team playing its first game.

"We've brought in four umpires from neighboring towns so there shouldn't be any prejudicial calls. Besides the man calling balls and strikes, we have two for the bases and for determining fair or foul once the ball has traveled past the first and third bases. The fourth will keep the official scorecard, unless he has to fill in if one of the other umpires gets hurt. We have left and right foul poles. Anything hitting the poles are foul balls and out of play. All rules, according to the Official National League Rulebook, will be duly enforced."

The two managers handed Larry Sanderson, the umpire offering to call balls and strikes, their scorecards. He put one from each coach in his back pocket. He then switched the remaining two cards and handed them back. The coaches took the returned cards and everyone turned facing a flag pole. That cued Beulah Metheney, the choir director for the Church of Christ, to commence singing "The Star Spangled Banner." The people in attendance stopped and, turning toward the flag, put their hands over their hearts.

At the end of the song Larry Sanderson, Mayor Bob's uncle, yelled, "Play ball."

The Dancing Deer players had allowed the visiting team to take their infield practice first and, after their own turn, they stayed on the field. David Blaine had been warming up his dad, so when the umpire said "Play Ball" he squatted behind the plate, took four more pitches, before throwing to second.

The first man up swung at the first pitch and missed by half a foot. He swung at the second pitch and was halfway through his swing when the ball slammed into David's mitt. The Polecat hitter stumbled out of the batter's box asking for time, took a few practice swings, and stepped back in. The next two pitches were low and called balls. Jed thought the second was a strike, but let it ride. The next pitch was an off-speed pitch and the batter hit a hard grounder straight at the hole between short and second. Daniel Poul played deep and had enough time and fast enough feet to get to the ball, scoop it up, and hurl it to first. The first out and the people in the stands stood, clapped, and hollered praise for a job well done.

The second batter went down swinging, and the third batter hit a line drive to left field. It got by the fielder and the runner made it all the way to third before the fielder could get the ball rounded up and thrown to the infield.

The next batter walked and promptly stole second. The fifth batter struck at three balls out of the strike zone and threw his bat down in disgust.

In the bottom of the first, Jesse announced, "First up for Dancing Deer is the shortstop, Daniel Poul." The crowd clapped their approval. Daniel popped to second. Paul Nelson promptly struck out, and Bear Radisson crowded the plate when it was his turn. He got hit and trotted to first. Leonard, the third baseman, struck out to end the inning.

The second, third, and fourth innings went all about the same. The Skunk Hollow Polecats got at least one or two walks per inning and a base hit. Sometime during their half of the inning, they usually popped-up for an easy out and two would go down swinging, with the last out leaving two or three men on base. The Men from Dancing Deer usually struck out, with only the occasional ground ball. They had no base hits.

David walked over to Jed in the bottom of the fourth inning. "Dad, everything their pitcher throws up's called a strike. We have to get our strike-outs through missed swings. If these people from Skunk Hollow weren't so aggressive, the blooming ump would walk them all. He's not calling a fair game. What can we do?"

"I think you're right. Bill's already said something, but I don't know unless he gets hoarse from all his bellowing and has to ask for a relief. So far we've been damn lucky. We're through four innings and they've left nine men on base. Sooner or later they're going to punch someone across and, it looks like, none of us can hit the damn ball. We should've taken more batting practice." At that moment they heard a loud crack of the bat and Bear Radisson lumbered past as fast as his three-hundred-pound frame could motor. Leonard walked on five pitches down in the dirt with one being called a strike.

It was David Blaine's turn to bat with two men on base. A left-hander, he was a mixed bag. He fielded as a rightie and batted like a leftie. From the right side of the plate David hit the first pitch over the third baseman's head. It wasn't hit well—pretty much off the end of the bat. The ball had a quirky spin and, although it landed in fair ground, it darted into the fans just outside the foul line. Two runs scored with David Blaine reaching third before the left fielder could retrieve the ball and get it into play.

The Skunk Hollow manager ran to the third-base umpire crying unfair. The three umpires conferred and decided Leonard should go back to third and David Blaine to second with one run scoring instead of two.

Leonard scored on a passed ball and David Blaine advanced to third. When Jed came to bat he hit a sharp single just over the second baseman's outstretched glove to score David Blaine. In the top of the fifth it was three to nothing with the Men from Dancing Deer in the lead.

The first man up for Skunk Hollow promptly got two strikes. He tried to check his swing on the third pitch, but to everybody it appeared he went around. The umpire behind the plate yelled, "Ball." The man walked.

With the count of two balls and one strike on the next batter, the runner tore off for second when Jed kicked to home. David threw a hard shot to the second baseman, but it bounced off his glove into right field, allowing the runner to advance to third. The next man struck out swinging and the next walked. The next hitter shot a hard grounder to short. Daniel Poul caught the ball, stepped on second, and threw a bullet to first. Paul Nelson caught the ball then dropped it, allowing the runner from third to score.

The following batter hit a long fly ball to left field. It was misplayed by the fielder and the hitter ran all the bases, making the game's first homerun. Jed struck out the next batter. Starting the bottom of the fifth inning, the Polecats had tied the score at three.

61

Dancing Deer didn't score in their half of the fifth, with three men going to the plate and three easy outs. Neither team scored in the sixth or seventh, with all six batters for Dancing Deer striking out. David was sure some of the called strikes were actually balls. He was getting more and more agitated with the umpire. When it was his turn to bat, he stood deep in the batter's box and swung at the first pitch without taking a step into it. Reaching back with the bat, he actually hit the catcher's glove, knocking it off his hand. The umpire called David out through interference. Old man Ridley stumbled out of the dugout with his rule book. He showed the umpire the reference and the umpire had no choice but to rescind the out and award David Blaine first base. The two succeeding batters struck out, leaving David stranded on first.

In the top half of the eighth Jed walked the first man on four straight pitches. The walked batter stole second on Jed's first pitch to the second batter. With the count at one ball and no strikes and the runner now on second, the batter squared to bunt. The ball rolled six feet in front of the plate and died. David grabbed the ball, checked third, pivoted, and threw to first. Paul Nelson caught the ball, but had neither foot on the bag. The umpire called the runner safe while the runner on second moved to third. Jed struck out the next batter. With runners on the corners, the next Polecat hit a weak roller to second. The runner from third made it home easily as Wally Braxton underhanded the ball toward second base. Daniel gracefully caught the ball and slid his foot deftly across the top of the bag before hurling it hard to first. He hoped on making a double play on the slow catcher plowing down the line. The ball was a little low and went through the legs of Paul Nelson. The runner went on to second. He scored on a line drive to left. When the inning was over the Polecats had jumped to a two-run lead.

Little Johnny Nelson came to the edge of the bench where his dad sat. "Dad, Timmy overheard his father talking to Mayor Bob. They're saying you're playing badly because you bet money that Skunk Hollow would win. It isn't so, is it, Dad?"

Three up and three down and the Men from Dancing Deer had to go back into the field for the top of the ninth and final inning still down by two. Jed informed David his arm was killing him and he didn't know if he'd be able to pitch much longer.

The first batter for Skunk Hollow hit a wicked grounder to first. All Paul Nelson could do was knock it down and toss it underhanded to Jed, who came sailing across first ahead of the runner. The second out was a line drive to Leonard who had to catch it out of self-defense. With two outs the third Polecat to come to the plate walked. David decided to give his dad the signal for a pitch-out. He knew the man on first would try to steal second on the first pitch. Hell, they'd been stealing all day. Jed pitched from the stretch, he came to set, gave a look to the runner on first, and kicked to the plate. The runner tore out for second. David Blaine jumped up and to the right of the batter for the pitch-out. He'd get this one. The ball screamed over the middle of the plate, waist high. The batter swung and missed. He later swore he saw steam coming out at the seams. The ball slammed into the midsection of the umpire.

David picked up the ball and tossed it to his father. The third-base official called time as several people scrambled in to see if the umpire behind the plate needed his last rites given. He lay in the prone position, holding his pants where a cup should have protected a vital area.

"Jerry, you going to be all right?"

With his eyes closed and with deep-creased furrows radiating outward from each he managed to gasp, "Damnit. They did that on purpose. Throw 'em out." He then rocked from side to side and tried to get up. Two men came with a stretcher and hauled him to the concession stand. A nurse said she needed to pack the hurt area with ice to keep the swelling to a manageable limit. Jerry Sanders moaned, "You plan on doing that in front of all these bystanders?"

The nurse unzipped Larry Sanders' pants. "We're all adults here. I'll just reach in with this handful of ice and . . ."

"Damnit, lady, leave me alone. Get your hand out of there."

Bill Potter, the opposing manager, and the three remaining officials, conferred at home plate. What was decided, over Bill's strong objection, was that both David Blaine and Jed had been tossed from the game as the last official act of the now-indisposed umpire. The umpire who had been keeping the official scorecard took over behind the plate calling balls and strikes. And Bill went to the bench for a glove.

"Mr. Ridley, can you still catch a ball?"

"Yeah, just can't run no more."

"Then sir, you got first."

Bill went to center while Bear Radisson moved to catcher. Daniel Poul trotted to the pitcher's mound and Paul Nelson ran to short. Bill didn't have extra players.

The batter expected a fast ball from the relief pitcher and was way ahead of the pitch. Daniel's toss was at least twenty miles per hour slower than Jed's. Daniel's second pitch was a curve and, since Jed had not thrown one, the batter looked silly missing when the ball swung wide after looking like it was going to be over the plate. Two balls later, Daniel threw up a lollypop. It was more like a girl's slow-pitch softball toss than something you'd see in a baseball game. The batter's timing was off, and all he could manage was a pop-up to shallow left field. Paul Nelson gauged the flight of the ball and turned his back to the infield. He ran hard toward the incoming right fielder. The ball was dropping fast. Paul took one last look over his right shoulder. In two more strides, without another look back, Paul reached his glove in front of his right shoulder. He caught the ball while still running and his back facing the infield. It was a miraculous grab—the greatest fielding effort of the entire game by either side.

Now it was Dancing Deer's last chance. They were down by two runs, and so far a single by Jed and another by Big Bear Radisson were the only decent Dancing Deer hits. Paul Nelson led off the inning. He missed badly on the first pitch and watched helplessly as the next three pitches skittered past. One was called a strike on the outside corner. With the count at two balls and two strikes, Paul, already with three strikeouts, squared to bunt. He had to get some wood on the ball. Instead of bunting, he punched hard at the ball and hit a decent grounder toward a charging third baseman. It went wide of his grasp and was fielded deep in the hole by the shortstop. Paul Nelson had his first base hit.

Big Bear Radisson came to the plate and, with his feet a little forward in the batter's box, he leaned farther forward just as the pitcher released the ball. The ball hit Bear on his arm hanging over the plate. The umpire awarded Bear first and the Skunk Hollow manager came charging out saying the ball was over the plate and should have been called a strike. He didn't win this argument, just as countless others before him routinely lost similar arguments to the umpire's original assessment.

The tying runs were now on base and it was Leonard's time to bat. Leonard had already struck out twice and hit a slow roller to the pitcher to account for his trips to the plate. This time, however, he hit a high fly ball to right field. It would have been a homerun if it had been fielded by Dancing Deer's right fielder, but Skunk Hollow's player backed up and caught the ball in a cavalier waist-high underhanded grab. The fans stood, but it was just a long out with Paul Nelson tagging on the catch and advancing to third.

Bill came to the plate for the first time. Dancing Deer was down by two runs and had runners on the corners. He fouled off several good pitches before finally walking to load the bases. Bill would be the winning run if he could cross the plate. Wally Braxton came to bat and fouled out to the first baseman.

So, with the bases juiced, two outs, and two runs behind, old man Ridley slowly walked over and picked up an old bat leaning against the fence.

The Skunk Hollow players laughed at the sight. Old man Ridley was ninety plus and more or less hobbled on short steps to the plate. Before stepping into the batter's box he took a practice swing. The catcher and umpire could hear his back popping as several vertebrae shifted places. He wasn't wearing the royal blue baseball cap that matched the Dancing Deer uniforms. No, his was with a short bill and of an indistinguishable color, more brown than black. Dimmed with age, an indecipherable emblem adorned the hat's crown. He took his stance with the bat held high, his two thin legs close together. The ball came in high and tight, brushing Mr. Ridley off the plate.

The catcher jumped up and ran to the mound.

"For God's sakes, don't hit him. That's what he wants. He's not going to strike at the ball. Hell, look how old he is. And if he's lucky enough to hit the ball, it'll be a slow dribbler with a play at every base."

Paul Nelson broke for home as the catcher started his walk back to home plate. Paul never saw the catcher ask for time, and timed his move to the next instant after the catcher handed the ball to the pitcher. The catcher didn't have as far to run, but he was severely hampered by his apparatus. Paul arrived at the plate a good two strides before the catcher, who didn't have the ball anyway.

The pitcher picked up the rosin bag. He bounced it in his pitching hand while waiting for his nerves to settle. His second pitch to Mr. Ridley kicked up dirt on Mr. Ridley's cleats. It skittered away from the catcher and both runners moved up. With first base now open, the pitcher didn't care if he walked the old man, so he threw the next two pitches over the outside corner. Both were called strikes. The next throw was the pitcher's four-seam fastball. It came in over the center of the plate. Old man Ridley made a gigantic effort. He had guessed the pitcher would be tossing his bread and butter fastball and the teetering old man was ready. He started his swing about the time the ball had traveled halfway between the rubber and the plate. When the ball crossed the plate it collided head-on with the fat part of a bat made ten years before the Civil War. Old man Ridley had played when the league used a ball later called a dead ball. It wasn't until the twenties and long after Mr. Ridley had been led out to pasture that the league reconfigured the ball to have a high compression cork center and tighter wrappings. Mr. Ridley followed through, curling around at the waist, and sending the livelier ball over the third baseman's head.

At first he didn't run. He watched as it streaked through the air, staying close to the line right over the third baseman's head. The third-base umpire ran onto the playing field facing right field with both hands extending in a gesture saying the ball was fair. Old man Ridley started for first at a slow trot. One slow step after another, not exactly a run, somewhere between a hobble and a stumble. His right leg had been the first to make the move to first base, but had to wait after each step for the slower left to drag along the ground never quit pulling up even.

Jed jumped up from the bench and started walking beside Mr. Ridley, saying. "Mr. Ridley, you've got to make it to first. Bear's already crossed and Bill's coming in now. They're the tying and winning runs, but you have to reach first or they don't count."

All the players from the Dancing Deer squad joined Jed and walked alongside Mr. Ridley, just outside the foul line, yelling encouragement.

After hobbling forty feet and stumbling forty feet, old man Ridley fell, the left foot had become useless and the right couldn't drag him along by itself. Mr. Ridley landed in a puff of dirt eight feet shy of first base. He stretched his hand for the bag, but was still several feet shy. He gasped for air as the fans descended from the stands and got as close as they could without venturing onto the playing field. They stared at the old man with open mouths, each trying to get a glimpse of their last hope. Some prayed, others pleaded, and still others begged old man Ridley to get to his feet and make the last piddling distance. He flailed at the ground. Finally, he pulled his legs up under him and used the bat he still carried to push his tired body up on its knees. He fell forward. His fingers now clawing the earth inches shy of the base when the ball made it back to the infield. A hundred people watched and yelled encouragement from close quarters as old man Ridley's strength ebbed away. He could not get those last few inches.

Torguson Ridley's eyes were glazed and spittle oozed from his mouth when the first baseman reached down and tagged out the game old man. The fans descended onto the field. They loved old man Ridley. He had given everything he had for them.

The first-base umpire yelled for everybody to clear a path. The fans backed off, leaving only the first baseman standing on the base holding the ball and old man Ridley prone on the ground with his hand stretched to its limit. His index finger was snugged against a piece of metal sticking up from the ground five inches short of the base.

The first-base umpire raised his hand to form a fist in the familiar signal designating an out then quickly lowered it and, bending over, looked to see what Mr. Ridley was touching. To the first baseman he asked, "Is your base attached to the ground?"

The first baseman said, "Yes, sir." and toed it with his shoe. The bag moved.

The umpire stood up. With his hands held out level with the ground, palms down he yelled, "Safe."

CHAPTER 14 – THE GALA

Faye talked Glenda into re-scheduling her two Friday standing appointments and hanging a "Closed for Repairs" sign on the glass front door. They would spend the day shopping. With the hundred dollars, Faye planned on purchasing an evening gown, matching shoes, and a small black purse. Glenda brought along some money as well, but she did not anticipate buying anything. She just wanted to be prepared in case she found something she couldn't live without.

After two hours on Fifth Avenue, Faye had purchased her purse. They stopped at a delicatessen for sandwiches. Faye figured she needed to find her dress and shoes in the next hour so Glenda would have time to style her hair. She found the dress in the second store after their meal and the shoes not long after. When they arrived back at Glenda's shop, Faye got out with three parcels and Glenda had spent all her money at the shoe store, purchasing six different pairs.

"I don't know why I buy so many shoes. I've got a closet-full as it is. Still, have you heard the saying 'Life's short, buy the shoes?'"

Glenda used the front door to help her hold the boxes as she used her one free hand to fumble in her purse for the keys. She unlocked the front door with only one box spilling its treasure of open-toed red heels to the concrete. It was Faye who held the door as Glenda negotiated the opening still carrying five boxes of shoes.

That evening a limousine picked up the chief and his date promptly at seven-thirty. Faye looked beautiful in an aqua-blue strapless gown. It was tight to the waist and free-flowing to the floor.

Chief Wainwright said, "Doll, you are too stunning for words." He helped her cover her bare shoulders with a cream-colored linen drape held together with a rhinestone clasp. Holding out his arm, he helped her through the front door for an evening on the town. "What are you going to do if you pop out of that snug-fitting top?"

"I don't know. But I've got this handsome date to shield me while I make a clothing adjustment. And I've got safety pins in my purse."

Their driver let out a low whistle as they approached the limo. It was the same driver who had chauffeured the mayor and the chief around since the mayor had shown up at the chief's second radio broadcast. Word had gotten around that a newcomer on the scene had some insightful ideas about fighting New York City's abundant crime. The mayor thought if the radio audience liked his ideas then he was a man to have in tow. W.W. and the mayor eventually became close friends with the mayor relying more and more on the chief's assessment of the city's problem.

A man in a tuxedo took their tickets at the front door and led them to their table. They were fashionably fifteen minutes late. Already seated were Maxine and her husband Jaime. He stood when their introduction was made and held out a small hand. Faye thought it was somewhat sweaty and quickly turned to the next guest. Faye could not make out many names as the room was alive, loud, and electric. She nodded and shook hands as Chief Wainwright made the introductions with a quaint and focused greeting for each.

When seated, Faye whispered to the chief, "How do you know all these people?"

"Politics is a small circle of influential people. I've seen their pictures in the papers. And I'd been given a seating chart with a line or two about each. I studied it for over an hour."

"W.W., you must've been a boy scout."

"Indeed I was. 'Always be prepared' is my motto. It's served me well in my thirty-five years in law enforcement."

The mayor arrived. People cleared a path, cameras flashed, and loud talk hushed to whispers as he strode through a sea of New York City's well-heeled. Everyone at his table, and indeed, everyone at every table stood. A waiter rushed to pull out his chair. Instead, he veered to his right and walked straight to Faye.

"My dear, you must be the beautiful woman our Arkansas' chief has been talking about. My name is Trevor Radix." He held out his hand.

"I am so glad you were able to come to our little get-together." Holding her hand he turned to the other people at his table. "During the course of the evening we need to get Miss Spencer to tell us of her big adventure. Please help me, for I am dying to know how she was kidnapped by a murderer and escaped after two weeks in captivity. Of course, she wrote a book and soon I'll be able to read about it, but, while we have her here, I say we pry it out."

There was suitable clapping. The mayor turned to Faye and said loud enough for everyone to hear, "Miss Spencer, there are two pesky publishers who wish to speak with you. Of course, we have Maxine and her husband Jaime right here at our table. I do hope you'll choose one of our New York City publishers. One of those wishing to talk with you is from New Jersey—almost a foreigner. Ha, ha."

While everyone laughed, Jaime said something under his breadth to Maxine. Maxine's face grew red as her husband's whisper developed harsh undertones.

After shaking hands all around, the mayor bounded onto the stage and, from the lectern, grabbed a microphone. Everyone once standing, now quickly found seats except the waiters, who worked at fast clips to make sure everyone had drinks. The mayor walked around the stage like an entertainer as he told his supporters how pleased he was to have such a splendid turn-out. He said he was humbled by the tremendous support he enjoyed and he wanted everyone to know that, during his second term in office, he would continue having an open-door policy. If a person had a problem, a complaint, was treated unjustly, or needed help, he and his subordinates would see to it that the city government bent over backwards to make sure each and every citizen would be heard and appropriate action provided.

He took a few well-chosen questions from planted supporters, made well-rehearsed replies to each, and then told everyone to enjoy their meal, to dance to the music, and to have a good time. As he was walking off the stage amid thunderous applause, someone in a white dinner jacket walked out from the wings and, through a microphone, suggested they toast their illustrious mayor. The applause continued but was now punctuated by the chinking of stemware.

When the mayor reached his table, he motioned for everyone there to sit. Amid the cacophony, Faye turned to the chief. "Do you know anything about those two publishers?"

"No. I think he was making that up to get the Critos squirming. I wouldn't be surprised if you were offered a contract tonight."

From down at the end of the table came, "Miss Spencer, were you frightened?"

Someone else asked, "Who was murdered?"

"Is the murderer the man Chief Wainwright said Arkansas has a man-hunt for?"

Another asked, "Miss Spencer, how did you escape?"

As Faye tried to answer their questions, she swelled with pride, thinking this was what she had hoped her trip to New York City would be like. She ate some sort of chicken and rice casserole, drank several glasses of white wine, and danced many times with Chief Wainwright and once with her new friend, Trevor Radix. While showing W.W. how to do the waltz, Jaime Crito said something to her over his wife's shoulder, but Faye couldn't understand what he said and ended up shaking her head.

During a lull in the festivities Maxine leaned forward and said, "Faye, why don't you bring your manuscript to the office tomorrow. Maybe, we can work something out."

"Maxine, have you ever heard of an auction? How does that work?"

"I don't think there'll be a need for an auction. Why don't you let me look at your manuscript and if it's something we can use I'll make you an offer as good as anything you could get through an auction."

"Maxine, I only have the one manuscript and now another publishing house has it. I have an appointment with them on Monday morning. I think I'll receive the manuscript back, as she's already asked me if I would be willing to make a few small changes. I expect to be given an offer."

"I wouldn't be too hasty about signing anything. It usually takes an agent several meetings to hash out the details covering the rights the author sells and those she retains."

"Yes, I have a little knowledge about publishing contracts. Do you pay royalty on net or retail?"

"Miss Spencer, how did you eat during your captivity?" asked a thin man with slicked black hair.

"Yeah, and I'd like to know why he handcuffed you to the radiator."

"Maxine, my fans are calling. How about I come by your office tomorrow afternoon? I promise not to sign anything until you've had a chance to read it."

"That's fantastic, Faye. Anytime after one works for me." Faye turned to answer the latest round of questions and Maxine gave her husband a swift elbow to his rib cage.

CHAPTER 15 – TEN MEN IN DEBT

Mayor Bob called an impromptu meeting. He used the Dancing Deer City Council Chambers even though he didn't want to discuss the city's business. He wanted to discuss their wagers with Bill Potter and what they should do about paying their debts. Bill Potter, their nemesis, and the turncoat, Paul Nelson, were not notified of the meeting.

"Gentlemen, all is lost. I drove my tractor over and left it in the bank's parking lot. I couldn't look Bill in the face. Has anyone paid his wager?"

Harold Greenleaf said, "Yeah, I had it in my pocket and forked it over at the end of the game. Just walked up and threw it at him. What's with Nelson, anyway? We'd have lost that game and won our money if he'd kept his cool. To tell you the truth, I didn't know he was that good. My wife baked a pecan pie and made me wait in the car while she carried it to his door."

From the end of the table came, "I made a loan. When I sell my crop I plan on paying it off. He'll get most of my profit this year. But I might pay just a part of it so I'll have enough left to plant winter wheat. Robert, we were so damned sure Skunk Hollow would win I bet a lot more than I could afford to lose."

"Me, too. I put up some land in Hector I inherited as collateral. If I don't figure out how to pay it off, Bill Potter's going to end up with my granddaddy's homestead."

"My wife found out about me using the stash she'd put back for the quilting machine. She's made my life hell. I'm now doing dishes and learning to iron."

"We got to figure something out. My boy's been sending me his Army pay for three years. He thinks he's going to have enough money to marry his high-school sweetheart and open a small-engine repair shop. When he gets back, I'll have to tell him I bet his money on a baseball game and lost."

"Rube, Johnston, and I took out loans for a thousand each. We didn't put up any collateral. We're thinking about defaulting, but we'll probably have to leave town."

Mayor Bob raised his hand for quiet. "I've come up with a plan. Gentlemen, have a look at this." He passed around copies of an article from the *Nashville Tennessean*.

With each looking at his copy Mayor Bob started reading.

"Yesterday, I fell in love with baseball again. Now that so many baseball giants are fighting in the war, the ones still here are performing in lackluster fashion. I had given up writing about baseball, except for the Negro League and the Women's League, until yesterday.

"A traveling troupe of barnstormers took on a team from the Israelite House of David. If my readers will think back, it was this same team of long-haired and bearded men from Benton Harbor, Michigan, dubbed 'Jesus Boys' by Satchel Page, who took a lady pitcher and beat the world-champion St. Louis Cardinals in 1933 before ten thousand fans in Sportsman's Park.

"True, Jackie Mitchell, their lady pitcher, has only a fair curve and not much speed on her fastball, but she did have all the necessary poise. She pitched one inning, not allowing a run. And she popped to short, played by Leo 'The Lip' Durocher, at her only time at bat. After that first inning, the 'Jesus Boys' were leading Dizzy Dean and the pride of St. Louis—our beloved Cardinals—four to zip. At the end of the game, those same bearded men and one pretty lady swaggered home having whipped the best in professional baseball eight to six.

"These same 'Jesus Boys' had their hands full with a game on their home field against the New York Hotshots, made up of Cuban immigrants, a gangling pitcher with a sweeping curve, and a home-grown catcher with a gun attached to his right shoulder. Yesterday, I witnessed a war on a ball field. Both pitchers provided command performances, with fifteen strikeouts for the beards and twelve for the Hotshots through the sixth inning. At this time, under sweltering heat, the pitchers started giving ground. Both pitchers began getting the ball up in the strike zone and the bats commenced to peel away their veneer. At first came singles, then solid smashes up the center or down the lines, finally homeruns. Two by the home team and two by a lad named James Paul—the catcher for the Hotshots. The Hotshots had one other homerun and led eight to seven in the bottom of the ninth. With one out, the batter struck out with the ball scooped out of the dirt by James Paul. The runner headed to first praying for a miracle. James Paul threw so hard to first the ball knocked off the first-baseman's mitt. Two singles later, the man praying for a miracle scored the tying run.

"In the top of the tenth, the 'Jesus Boys' brought in a fresh pitcher, and he held the Hotshots to a few scattered singles for the next four innings. The Hotshots pitcher got slower and slower, but his curve was breaking more and more with their catcher using his body to block un-catchable tosses. Anything getting by him would squirt all the way to the backstop allowing any runner on base to advance. The game ended after thirteen innings tied at eight.

"Some say it was called because of impending darkness, but I believe the men didn't have any more to give. I love this game and I love those men. They put it all on the line, making heroic catches, stellar pitching performances, and clutch hitting. Baseball is America's game and I saw it at its best yesterday."

Mayor Bob sat down to a stunned group of men. "Gentlemen, if Skunk Hollow was anywhere close to the caliber of either of these two teams, we'd be at the bank right now gloating over our winnings."

"Do you think they'd come here to play the Peckerwoods?"

"The men from the Israelite House of David play most of their games on their own turf, but the Hotshots might be induced to travel here."

Harold Greenleaf stood up, "Send them boys a telegram and ask what they need to include us on their itinerary."

"Even if they came does anyone think Bill would be gullible enough to put it all on the line one more time—this time against a team so good?"

"Remember how mad he got when we referred to the town team as the Dancing Deer Peckerwoods?"

"Yeah."

"Well, we just need to needle him until his civic pride short-circuits his better judgment."

CHAPTER 16 – THE SECOND WAGER

A teary-eyed Faye Spencer sat in her seat looking out the window as the train wound through the countryside. She had a publishing contract for her book, a sizeable advance on her royalties, and a damp handkerchief. She started crying the moment the Dancing Deer Chief of Police, W.W. Wainwright, told her he wouldn't be accompanying her home. It looked like the mayor was going to win his election by a landslide and he'd offered the position of chief of police for New York City to his new protégé—and the soul-mate Faye had been hiding from for years as she focused on her career. She always knew there was someone out there for her. A man who would sweep her off her feet, transport her to paradise, and father her children. She had not expected that man to be twenty years older and four inches shorter than she. And leading a life fraught with danger. But it happened. A handsome man with a glint in his eye, a bounce in his step, and a gentle touch stepped into her life and swept her away to America's premier city. Now she was running back to safety.

W.W. asked her to stay, but she couldn't. Her home was in Arkansas. She loved her job, she loved being with her sister, and she loved the little town of Dancing Deer. Why couldn't he come back with her and be the chief of police there? She knew the answer. What would she have said if *The New York Times* asked her to be their star reporter with a salary forty times what Jesse was paying? Could she have said no? It would mean putting her career ahead of getting married, ahead of starting a family. Was it that important? She didn't let W.W. know her true feelings. When he asked her to stay, she laughed. When he said he loved her, she laughed. When he said he wanted to get married, she laughed. She wasn't laughing now.

"Bill, you got a minute?" Jellico, Dancing Deer's prominent attorney—the same one who had represented Bill in his trial for the murder of Raylene Carlisle and Galen Hamelin—stood in Bill's outer office.

"Sure, Jellico. What's up?"

"It's old man Ridley. He's dying, Bill. The doctor said he had a heart attack running to first in the ball game. He thinks the old man might have a few more months, but he won't make it to the end of the year."

"That's too bad. He was something. Knocked that ball to Cleveland, but his legs couldn't get his body ninety feet. Well, ninety-one feet. As he plainly displayed, he did make it ninety feet, but not an inch farther."

"Bill, how the hell did he find the base peg stuck in the ground?"

"I don't know. It's just one of those mysteries that makes life so enjoyable."

"Well, I'm here because Mr. Ridley has decided to give the town a parcel of land adjacent to City Park. He wants a baseball field built. He's even putting up the money for its construction. Do you think the city council will have any problem accepting? I know they've built up a considerable amount of angst against our anonymous donor and his gifts to the town."

"No, I've got the city council in my back pocket. Actually their butts are in Carla's desk drawer. They won't be giving any more problems."

"I see. No, I don't see, but I also don't care. I've got my hands full with Sheriff Shodtoe's trial. I'm filling my spare moments drawing up the papers for the ballpark. Do you think you could inform the city council at their next meeting?"

Bill stood at his chair. "Gentlemen, Mr. Ridley is planning on building a baseball stadium next to City Park. After it's built and named Ridley Field, he wants to donate it to the city. I suggest we accept with gratitude. Perhaps we could show our appreciation by blocking off Main Street and throwing a shindig in his honor. Mayor Bob, ask if someone will second my motion."

Paul Nelson yelled out, "I second it."

Mayor Bob asked all those in favor of Bill's motion to raise their right hands. With Bill glaring around the room, first at one council member and then at another, the hands started raising. Soon, to Bill's approval, every hand was suspended at eye level.

Mayor Bob stood holding a letter he'd received. "Council members, let's move on. Dancing Deer's Peckerwoods have received another challenge. This one comes from a traveling troupe of barnstormers called the New York Hotshots. They want to play us on Labor Day and offers the town two thousand dollars if we can beat 'em."

Paul Nelson piped up, "We're not the Dancing Deer Peckerwoods."

"No? Well, who are we?"

"No one's come up with a name yet. We've just been calling ourselves the Men from Dancing Deer."

"Well, until the town can name their team I guess the fans can call them anything they want."

Bill stood up. "I think the term 'Peckerwoods' is a derogatory term. This team of ballplayers is a disciplined group of men who have shown they are fit to represent Dancing Deer and deserve to be treated with the respect they won against the Polecats from Skunk Hollow."

"Bill, are you saying our boys can hold a candle to these Hotshots?"

"Well, we were lucky the first time, but we played with a lot of heart and made the city proud. We might not win, but we'd give them a damn good game."

"I say the Peckerwoods wouldn't have a prayer against a decent team. Those Polecats were just what their name implied. I don't know why we thought they would be a worthy opponent. A good high school team could've beat them. And why did their pitcher lob that ball down the middle to old man Ridley. Hell, I could have hit it. As it was, the only reason it made it past the left fielder was because it hugged the foul line."

"Whoa, are you gentlemen asking to settle your debts with another wager?"

"Do you think our boys could win against a decent team?"

"I don't know, but since I've only received a run-down tractor and a thousand dollars thrown in the dirt, I have to believe the majority of you gentlemen are welchers. If you would be willing to put up something other than money, I might be willing to counter with your earlier losses."

"What do you have in mind?"

"Mayor Bob, you owe me seven hundred dollars. If our boys lose, I'll cancel the debt and give your tractor back. If we win, I think you, your wife, and both daughters should shell and can five hundred pounds of purple-hull peas. Another family could shuck and can five hundred pounds of corn. A third family could man a pantry I want to set up for dispensing food to the poor this winter. We could have it open three days a week till noon all winter. Are you gentlemen willing to wager a little work against your debts." Bill looked around the room.

"Let me make that a little more urgent. If you disagree then I'll give you another two weeks to bring me your money or I'll foreclose on the collateral. And I'll make a statement for the paper. How do you think the town will take it if they learn the city council—the men they've placed in charge of city business—bet against the same town they've sworn to manage and promote."

"Now, Bill, I for one haven't called the team the Peckerwoods."

"It doesn't matter. You've thrown in your lot and now you have to live with your choice."

Mayor Bob said, "I agree. Five hundred pounds of peas shelled and canned if the Peckerwoods prevail and my tractor back and marker torn up if they don't." Mayor Bob looked down at his feet. "What the hell. My wife loves to can."

Harold Greenleaf said, "I don't owe you any money. I'll bet you two thousand dollars even up. But you got to promise not to tell anyone. Especially Jesse Bell . . . and . . . uh, my wife."

"Agreed."

"What about the rest of us?"

"Give me a couple of days. I'll come up with a dozen or so civic projects and you can have your pick. I'll need everyone to sign an agreement. Mayor Bob, you may come to the bank and pick up your tractor after you've signed. I'll bring the list and blank agreements to our next meeting. The only stipulation is that you have your entire family participate, even the little ones—except for infants. And everything has to be finished by Christmas."

Mayor Bob held up his hand as everyone started talking at once. "Gentlemen, do we all agree?"

Paul Nelson said, "I don't."

Everyone turned in his direction.

"I lost five hundred dollars and don't want to ever bet against our town again. I played as hard as I could in the last one and will do so next time and the time after that and every time I represent our town in anything. You'll never again get me to bet against the town I love. In addition, I'm my son's hero and I wouldn't jeopardize that for all the tea in China."

"And for your loyalty, our anonymous donor has agreed to pay your five hundred dollars. Just thought you'd like to know."

"He knew about my wager?"

"It's the one made by Roger wasn't it?"

"Yeah."

"It's been paid."

"Harriet, you can't go. I need you."

"Oh, Willie, you don't know how much I've wanted to hear you say that."

"Our town's been challenged to another ball game and no one knows baseball better than you."

"You want me to help you with your ball team?"

"Yeah. What do you say?"

Bill looked at his estranged wife. It appeared that she was choking on something. "Harriet, are you okay?"

"No, Willie, I'm not. How much penance do I have to do? Why can't you love me like you once did?"

"I still love you. It wasn't me running off—leaving the marriage up in the air. You've now done that to me twice. This last time with an elderly Frenchman. You only came back to see me publicly humiliated."

"I did not. I received a telegram saying you bet your bank the town was going to win a baseball game. It said I should come back if I expected anything when our divorce became final."

"Who was it from?"

"Don't know. It didn't say. And what's more I didn't come back to gloat or even to salvage anything of value that might someday be mine. I came back because I wanted to help you. To be a part of your life again. I only went with Pepe when you said you loved Faye Spencer." Tears started streaming down her cheeks. She turned and ran through the lobby of the hotel to the elevator.

Bill walked to the staircase door. On the way, he told the concierge to stop the elevator at the second floor for two minutes while he ascended the stairs. When the elevator finally made it to the third floor Harriet stumbled out into the arms of her husband.

"How did you do that?"

"I'm a man of many talents."

"Yeah, well let me go. I'm going back to Boston."

"Harriet, have dinner with me. We can discuss everything and reach an understanding agreeable to both of us."

"Damnit, Willie, does everything have to be calculated? Can't you let emotion rule the day for once? I've been baring my heart to you and you're talking about agreements, contracts, challenges. Willie, I can't take it anymore."

"Okay. You talk and I'll listen. Go to your room, freshen up. Dress for dinner. I'll see you at eight and try my best to see things from your point of view."

CHAPTER 17 – HARRIET'S OPPORTUNITY

Pepe left for Florida. Harriet thanked him for a wonderful time, but said she needed to stay in Dancing Deer and, one more time, see if she could piece her marriage back together.

Pepe tried to ask Katy if she would accompany him for the remainder of his journey, but since she didn't speak French and he didn't speak English it was a useless waste of time. He kissed her, gave an affectionate hug, and patted her where only a paramour should have been allowed rights. He left a bewildered woman wondering what had just happened.

Pepe left Dancing Deer in his eight cylinder Duesenberg, with the top down, and a map of the southern states written over in French by his daughter. He'd memorized enough English words to order a decent meal; he knew a dozen or so he could use for asking directions; and another few that would get his face slapped. He had a sack-full of American currency and an over-flowing adventurous spirit. He promised Genevieve he'd be back by Christmas. He'd have plenty of time to see the tobacco fields in Virginia, the colonial mansions and brick roads in Charleston and Savannah, and the vast openness of the Gulf of Mexico. In Miami he wanted to watch Cubans hand-craft cigars, take an air-boat through the Everglades, and wrestle an alligator. No, not wrestle an alligator. But he did want to visit one of their sanctuaries at feeding time.

He'd be back at Christmas and then on to France. He had now written Odette ten letters. He'd received no reply, but then again to where would she send it? To the Duesenberg? Pepe laughed.

"Harriet, have you ever heard of the New York Hotshots?"

"No. But they can't be all that good. They're from New York, for God's sakes."

"So tell me, why do the people in Boston have such a fierce rivalry with the people of New York?"

"We built the greatest baseball stadium in the world, but we put it in New York City."

"I don't understand."

"Willie, you lived with me in Boston, but you never became a Bostonian. Fenway Park is a wonderful stadium. It's cozy, with the fans feeling like they're almost on the field. And then there's the 'Green Monster,' but Yankee Stadium is in a class by itself." Harriet unfolded her napkin and set it in her lap. From the bread tray she retrieved a slice of black bread.

"For the first fifty years, baseball was dominated by great pitching and superhuman defenses. You ever heard 'Tinker to Evers to Chance?'"

"No."

"These are the saddest of possible words
    Tinker to Evers to Chance.
    Trio of Bear Cubs and fleeter than birds
    Tinker to Evers to Chance.
Thoughtlessly pricking our gonfalon bubble,
    Making a Giant hit into a double,
    Words that are weighty with nothing but trouble,
    Tinker to Evers to Chance."

Bill pulled on his ear. "No, I've never heard of them before."

"They were the short to second to first double-play infielders of one of the greatest baseball teams in history—the Chicago Cubs of the early 1900s. And Ty Cobb's precision hitting for Detroit gave him a lifetime batting average of three sixty-seven. It was the time of the short game: singles, doubles, bunts, stolen bases. No one hit many homeruns. League leaders belted out only ten to fifteen all year. Then the Black Sox Scandal of 1919 put America off baseball.

"At about that time we had a bandy-legged pitcher by the name of George Herman Ruth. He was a wonderful pitcher who was also good with the bat. Harry Frazee, the owner of our team during those days, was more interested in financing Broadway plays than in fielding a good baseball team. What started out as a team many considered the best in baseball was sold off piecemeal to Jacob Ruppert of New York.

It was called 'The Rape of the Red Sox.' One of the sales was our best pitcher.

"They, the New Yorkers, correctly figured that baseball needed a new road to travel, so after making Ruth's purchase the Yankees moved him to the outfield where he could play every day. He rewarded them with tape-measure shots. Ruth hit fifty-four homeruns his first year with the Yankees, twice the number anyone had ever hit before. It brought back the fans and they used his drawing power to build Yankee Stadium. It's called 'The house that Ruth built.' The 'Big Bambino' knocked a game-winning homerun on Yankee Stadium's opening day. He never looked back and we never forgave the owner of our team. We also never forgave the New Yorkers for taking advantage of Frazee's stupidity."

"Harriet, do you think the Men from Dancing Deer could beat a team—say a team about as good as an average minor league team?"

"Not in a million years."

"Damn. I bet your share of what I'm worth that we could."

"What are you talking about?"

"Oh, forget it. Its only money. You've got enough clothes to last you several years. Why, you could get a job, pick up the slack, so to speak. Live here where it doesn't cost that much, rent an apartment. You'd be just fine."

"You're crazy. I've never worked. I attend parties. People take care of me. I'd give all that up if it meant getting your forgiveness, but having to get a job. I'd have to think about that."

"If you were to take two months and manage our baseball team to where it put up a good fight against a New York team—no, to where it beat a New York team, then you wouldn't have to worry. The town would carry you around on its shoulders—except for ten men. You could have anything you wanted."

"Anything?"

"Anything. Unless it put me in the poorhouse."

"Okay. So I could have anything I wanted as long as your financial integrity remained intact?"

"Yes. Absolutely."

"I'd have to have that in writing."

"You got it, but it only happens if you actually win the game. It's on Labor Day and I understand they are fairly good."

"Will you supply me with working capital? I'll need some new equipment."

"You can have whatever you need."

"How about a hundred dollars per week for the players so they can focus on the game and not have to worry about holding down regular jobs?"

Bill did some quick calculations. "I've only got nine players other than myself and we got seven weeks. Yeah. I'll even agree to that."

"I want one more thing. I want each player to have a room in the hotel for the entire seven weeks. A private room so his wife and kids can stay with him."

"Harriet, honey, this is getting out of hand."

"Willie, how bad do you want to win the game?"

"Pretty damn bad. Okay. Okay. Anything else?"

"No. That'll do it. Now let's talk about us."

"What about us?"

"Willie, do you ever think about me?"

"Sure I do."

"In a romantic way?"

Bill was now squirming in his seat. He was comfortable in stocks, bonds, convertible debentures. He dealt with logical issues. The emotional side of his brain, short of nurture, had somehow withered. Sure, he thought of Harriet. She was a beautiful woman with a lot of energy. She caused things to happen. He had loved her and their life together. In fact, he still loved her, but he was not about to let her lead him on and then jump ship like she had done two times already.

"Harriet, do you need a boyfriend, a sugar-daddy?"

"What?"

"Do you need someone to take care of you, someone to love you, someone to provide for you, or on the other hand do you need someone for you to love and to take care of?"

"I want you to love me, Willie."

Bill decided he needed to think about this and sprinkled salt over his potatoes. From the steak he plucked a little stick telling the waiter how well-done it was, and from the bread-tray he took a slice of hot pumpernickel to butter. Bill looked into the questioning eyes of his second love. Emily had been his first, but Jed Calhoun married her. Harriet came along during his college years. After a brief period of intense dating, Bill found her father and two brothers at his doorstep. After a brief talk he had been convinced that to marry Harriet was in his best interest.

"Willie, do you not have anything to say?"

"I'm thinking. Do you still wear those short see-through nighties?"

"Not lately, but I could."

CHAPTER 18 – THE ANNOUNCEMENT

The citizens of Dancing Deer first heard about the upcoming game with the New York Hotshots from their semi-weekly newspaper, the *Marsden County Meteor*. From the Associated Press, Jesse found enough material on their future opponents to put the fear of the Divine Being into his readership. The article said the Hotshots' record was forty-seven, zero, and one. They had never been beaten and tied only once.

So far the citizens of Dancing Deer had not thought it important enough to actually name their team. The players on the team referred to themselves as the ball team or the Men from Dancing Deer, but there were others who happened to overhear the team being referred to as the Peckerwoods and passed it on. Now half of the town was calling the team the Dancing Deer Peckerwoods, a fourth didn't care what they were called, and the last fourth was appalled that the pride of their town would be saddled with such an undignified moniker.

The players were telephoned by Bill's secretary and dutifully showed up at the Ritz Grand Hotel and Ballroom on the first evening after Bill and Harriet made their agreement. They brought their wives or girlfriends and, for one player, a boy of eight. This was the evening before Jesse's paper would tell the town what a large problem lay before their town heroes. Tonight the town's heroes would celebrate a job well done.

In a conference room decorated with balloons, blown-up pictures, and piped-in music the celebrants sat along a table with Bill and Harriet at one end. To their right sat Bill and Harriet's daughter, Rose, and her husband, David Blaine Calhoun. At the other end sat Paul Nelson, his wife, and little boy.

Bill stood up and raised his glass. "I just want to tell you how proud I am of the team's performance. It looked like we were in over our heads, but we stuck to it and with the help of one old man we squeaked by. That old man is too sick to attend this celebration, but, in his honor, I would like to propose a toast." Bill raised his glass. "Mr. Ridley, here's to you, sir. You are the example by which we walk."

Bill proceeded to down his drink as his guests agreed, clapped, and cheered, "Here's to you, Mr. Ridley."

"Gentlemen and ladies, I took the liberty of asking Andre to prepare Texas T-bones for the gentlemen and bacon-wrapped filets for the women. Dishes of salads, potatoes, and vegetables will be brought out and spread over the table. I have also told the waiters to keep the glasses full. After the meal I thought we'd go into the ballroom where a magician will perform.

"I know this little get-together was hastily prepared, but as my secretary told you, things are happening fast. Before we eat does anyone have a comment on the game?"

"I do." Leonard raised his hand. "Why was the umpire behind the plate calling balls and strikes in the Polecat's favor?"

"Yeah, everyone noticed it. People sitting behind where the Polecat players were standing could hear them laughing about it."

"That Larry Sanderson better not come into my dad's shop for a haircut. He might leave with only one ear."

"Gentlemen, he was just an obstacle we had to overcome. Somewhere, someday, he'll receive his reward."

"Some people think he's already received it. Jed, did you offer to autograph the reward?" There was quite a bit of laughing and stemware chinking on this admonishment.

"I've heard we might have another game on the horizon. Bill, you know anything about that?"

"Yes, that's the reason Carla had to hurry this along. Tomorrow the paper will have an announcement that we've been challenged to another game."

"That's great."

"Fantastic."

"Bring 'em on."

Bill waited through the clapping, the back-slapping, and the tinkling of glasses as toasts were exchanged around the table. "Gentlemen, these guys are semi-pro. They've offered us a reward of two thousand dollars if we can beat them. They don't expect to lose. In fact, they've been playing all summer and no one's beaten them yet."

"They haven't faced a pitcher like Jed Calhoun yet."

"Ha, ha." Everyone laughed except Jed, who turned several shades of red.

"They've won forty-seven games. At least ten of those games have been against all-star teams. That's where several towns got together to pool their best players. No one's come close. I don't want to scare you guys, but we might get humiliated. It might be like Mayor Bob going against Joe Luis in a boxing match." Bill looked around the table. Every eye looked back. "What I would like to know is whether or not we're big enough to be pummeled by a superior team and still give the game our best shot without resorting to excuses, apologies, or outbursts of indignation."

From the center of the table Bear Radisson said, "Do you think we can't beat them?"

"I'm willing to do everything I can to bring a victory to fruition. And I've got to tell you, I have an ace up my sleeve. But, going into this, everyone's got to know that their team is only a shade shy of the New York Giants."

"Good God!"

"I think it's worth the effort. I, for one, want to give it a go."

"Me, too."

"I'm in."

A woman's voice called from the end of the table. "Wally will be there."

"And my dad."

"Okay. Okay. It's unanimous. For now let's eat, drink, and be merry for tomorrow we . . . uh . . . we play the Hotshots."

There was thunderous applause.

"Okay, a few more items before we dig in. During the next two months, everyone will be in training. Your meals will be provided by Andre and you'll be living here . . . everything at my expense." Bill produced a sack of keys. "Each of you will be given a private room so your family can stay with you, if that's what you want. And to compensate for lost wages, or to find someone to do your work, I'm giving everyone a hundred dollars per week. Take the day off tomorrow.

Get everything set up and be here in the evening by seven. Curfew is at nine because we start practice at daybreak every morning thereafter."

CHAPTER 19 – HARRIET IN CHARGE

"Gentlemen, have a seat. This is our strategy room." Harriet held the door open. "Here we are going to learn baseball by the book. And here is the book. One for each person."

Harriet started handing out three-ring binders. "There's a box of pencils by the door and a sharpener bolted to the wall by the light switch. Each of you will be responsible to know everything possible about the position you play and quite a bit about every other position. Most of it is written in your book. If we discuss something not in the book, you'll have to add it. It'll take us playing our very best, knowing everything in these books, and having a bucket of luck to even make this game interesting. The chances of our team, with one game under its belt, beating someone like the New York Hotshots is astronomical."

Harriet walked to the front of the room. "Gentlemen, this is where we start to whittle away at those odds. Everyone head to the bistro for breakfast. Come back here in thirty minutes. Today we're going over the rules. That's all. Thirty minutes, men."

As everyone started heading for the door Harriet added, "Jed, could you and David Blaine stay for a minute?"

After the other eight men filed out Harriet said, "I'll bet nobody thought they'd have a woman as their manager."

"Someone's got to be in charge. Bill says you're the ace up his sleeve, so we decided to listen to what you have to say."

"Sounds fair enough. You got anything to add, David?"

"No, ma'am."

"Okay. Jed, you did a wonderful job pitching against the Polecats. The first few innings they were only able to hit the ball when you tried to throw something off-speed. Either of you know how they knew something hittable was heading their way?"

"No? Well, Jed, you were telegraphing. With a slower windup and a slower delivery, you told them. But they still had a hard time hitting it because your accuracy allowed you to paint the corners. They knew it was something they would need to swing at, but it was either inside, tying up their hands, or low and away so they only got the end of the bat on it. Then in the sixth your arm starting giving you problems. By the eighth it hurt so bad you couldn't get your windup over your head and you started coming in three-quarter side-arm."

"You're a very observant woman. What do you think I can do to improve?"

"That's easy. Add another pitch to your fastball. And slow down that scorcher so you can throw for the entire game. Let's say you start making it come in at ninety or so. If you use the same windup, the same delivery, the same arm speed, and every once in a while the ball came in at seventy-five, you'd be devastating. The batter's timing would be off. He wouldn't know when to start his swing. Of course, David Blaine would call the pitches. You're out there concentrating on pitching. There's the runners, all these thoughts about wind-up, delivery, fielding, mechanics. You couldn't handle all that and who is up to bat or what he did last time up. That's the catcher's job."

"So how do I learn to throw an off-speed pitch?"

"That's what I'm going to teach you. And movement. If the hitter is a seasoned ball player and decent at the plate he will hit a fastball that comes in without movement ninety percent of the time—if it's over the plate. But a fastball that rises or sinks in the last six feet before crossing the plate is another story. I can show you how to throw a two-seam fastball that sinks. And how to release the ball a little bit differently so your four-seamer rises. There are some scientists who think a ball can't rise because gravity counters anything air can do to the stitching, but if the batter is subconsciously expecting the ball to be gradually dropping and it stays level it makes the appearance of rising and he swings under it. We can also monkey around with a split-finger fastball, a slider, or a curve. But mainly we need one other pitch you can throw for a strike any time along with the fastball. If a third pitch works, so much the better, but one other for sure. We'll start work on it this afternoon."

Harriet's father had been a minor-league coach. He spent a big portion of his earlier years immersed in the trappings of America's game. Harriet decided it was time to call in her big gun.

When practice was over for the day and everyone had eaten and retired to their rooms, Harriet filled her iron claw bathtub to the brim with hot water and lilac-scented bath beads. When her body acclimated to the water, Harriet placed a telephone call to her home in Boston.

"Hello, Mom."

"Young lady, its about time you called. We heard from Bill that you headed west with a Frenchman. He said he was worried, but I told him you could handle yourself, thank you. So what's it like to be with an honest-to-God Frenchman? Did he kiss your hand? Just how do they kiss?"

"Oh, Mom, you've always been the romantic. He's just like any other man—except more of a gentleman. Is Dad around? I need to ask him for a favor."

"He's right here, trying to listen in on our conversation. Can't you tell me any more about the Frenchman?"

"Let me speak with Dad first, then I'll tell you what the French do when they take a lady out on the town."

"Tell me first, then I'll turn over the phone to His Highness."

"All right. They like to go to operas. When we were in San Francisco, we saw the most wonderful opera. We had to go shopping for clothes first. He bought himself a tuxedo and me a floor-length gown. The opera was sung in French. He was in heaven. It was about a woman married to a much older man. The marriage was arranged and there was no love between the two. Then a handsome man appeared and she was strangely attracted at first glance. They fell in love and contrived to poison her husband. After the deed was done and they had consummated their love for each other, they found out he was her long-lost brother. The man ran off and the woman had to come to grips with what she had done. Men are all the same, aren't they? When the going gets rough they get going. Can I talk to Dad now?"

"Yes, on both counts."

"Dad, you're going to have to take Mom out more. She seems starved for attention. Have you two stopped going to the theater?"

"Pumpkin, you know your mother. She's the one who decides where we go and what we do. We probably attend one ball every weekend. Then sometime during the week we have friends over for cards or go to one of their houses. I don't get a day off. Go to the theater? I've been driving her to New York City whenever a new play opens on Broadway. You got things backwards. You need to be telling her she needs to give me a break."

"So sorry, Dad. I should have known better. But the reason I called is that I need a scouting report on a team of barnstormers called the New York Hotshots. Have you ever heard of them?"

"A little bit. Weldon Simmons did a piece on them a couple of months back when they played the 'Jesus Boys.' Seems like they got a good pitcher and a damn good defense. Not much hitting though. You thinking about joining up and being their first base?"

"No. I'm managing the Men from Dancing Deer. We got a game against them on Labor Day and I want to know what their weaknesses are."

"You're managing a baseball team?"

"Yeah."

"Well, I'll be. My little girl wearing a ball uniform."

"So, Dad, can you help me out? We got a good pitcher and not much else."

"Honey, I've been out of baseball for ten years. Most of my contacts are also gone, but I'll do what I can. While I'm getting you the skinny on the Hotshots you better be working on your guys so they can hit the curve."

The next day at practice Harriet had Daniel Poul take the mound for batting practice. "Daniel, throw curves. Throw some overhand and some side-arm. Throw big sweeping curves and some little dinky curves. Let me know when your arm gets the least bit tired, cause we're going to do this every day."

"David Blaine, we got to get you a hinged catcher's mitt. A big, hinged catcher's mitt."

For the next two hours every man tried his luck hitting Daniel's curve ball. After lunch they went to the strategy room and talked about the mechanics of a curve ball—how it was thrown and what to look for in the windup or the way the pitcher held the ball tipping off the batter that a curve ball would be tossed. And how to get some wood on the elusive sphere.

"First of all, you've got to get over the fear of being hit. A curve won't travel with the same velocity as a fastball, so if you get hit, it'll just sting for a bit. So now, if you've decided the pitcher's going to throw a curve ball and its coming straight at you, then it'll break over the plate, so stay in there and swing at it. If it looks like its going over the plate, don't waste your energy. By the time it makes it to the plate, it'll be low and away. If you hold up, the umpire will call it a ball. When the pitcher gets down in the count, he'll have to throw something he's sure he can get over the plate and that's the one you hit.

"Walter Johnson—the Big Train—was dealt a terrible blow when he signed with Washington. He had amazing talent, but with no run support he never won as many games as he could have. Still, he had more than one year with thirty plus wins—with no support. He had a decent curve, a blistering fastball, and good control. He was also a nice guy, hardly ever brushing anyone back. Few men could effectively hit the Big Train—except Ty Cobb. Cobb said he would crowd the plate with his toes almost touching. He knew Johnson wouldn't hit him and would compensate for him crowding the plate by trying to throw the ball over the outside corner, a hard spot to paint. After getting down in the count with two balls and no strikes, Johnson would have to rely on his fastball somewhere in the strike zone. Cobb said that was the pitch he was waiting for. No one could hit Walter Johnson like Ty Cobb.

"I've heard that the pitcher for the Hotshots is known for a wicked curve. So that's what we're gonna learn to hit. Tomorrow we're gonna learn the mechanics of bunting. If you can't swing and hit it, then we'll find another way to get some wood on it.

"In the morning your gloves should be back. I had Jacoby's Leather Harness and Shoes lace the tops of the fingers together. Used to, people thought a glove softened the blow to the hand and made them to look like an oversized hand. Just like with your bare hand, you had to catch the ball in the palm, your other hand kept it from popping out. Now some smart people think the ball should be caught more between the forefinger and thumb. New gloves are coming out that lace the fingers together, have leather straps between the thumb and forefinger, and hinged between the little finger and palm. Jacoby's leather repair shop is adding the leather strapping and finger laces. We'll have to oil the hinge. I've heard the Indians chewed on their leather to get it soft and pliable. Any of you guys know what a good leather sandwich tastes like?"

"Yeah."

"You do?"

"Yeah, that's how my girl cooks. Everything she fixes tastes like leather."

There was general laughter as Harriet told everyone to get plenty of sleep because tomorrow they tackle the curveball.

During the next two months the Men from Dancing Deer studied the fundamentals for two hours after breakfast, and they studied strategy for two hours after lunch. The remaining ten hours of good daylight, they practiced on the field what they learned from the book. Every day they practiced hitting the curve ball and occasionally the fast ball—two kinds of fastball—from Jed. Eventually they could hit Daniel's curve, but no one could hit Jed's two fastballs. They practiced double plays every way one could be made. They learned how to bunt, how to steal bases, how to play the hit-and-run, and how to get into their opponents' heads to figure out what he would do next. The team was developing.

CHAPTER 20 – KATY BAR THE DOOR

"Lady, I ain't going nowhere. Haven't you heard? We're in training. We got a big game in less than two months against a team from New York City. It's the Civil War all over again. No one could drag me away before I get a chance to avenge my great-grandfather. I aim to whip 'em by myself, if need be."

Katy adjusted her notepad and flipped a page. "Mr. Poul, Mr. Jellico thinks the brother of your cellmate killed Raylene. That subpoena just asks for your presence at the trial. I'll let you know the day you'll be called to the stand. There's no need to interfere with your practice except for that one day. By the way, how good is Bill's wife as a baseball coach?"

"She's great. It's a shame she's a dame. We didn't much like being told we were less than mediocre, but she's shown us where we're weak and we're working on it. Do you know anything about old man Ridley?"

"Just that he can't get out of bed. Jesse Bell has to report to him every day about your progress. I wish we could get him to the game. The doctor says it would kill him. Still, I'll bet he'd make the trade."

"So, what's Mr. Jellico going to ask me? I've already owned up to the money."

"I think he'll focus on your cellmate. I'm headed out to the Tucker Farm tomorrow morning. Is there any information you can give me that might shed light on Gleason telling Evan about that money?"

"Whew. He's a mean one. I still owe him gambling money. There's no way I'll have to confront him, is there?"

"I'll tell Mr. Jellico to question you on different days. How's that?"

"That makes me feel better. He always had to go to the clinic when he was assigned a work detail. They'd give him a job like sharpening hoes or feeding the livestock and he'd spend the day vomiting. I think he might actually be allergic to work. Anyway, they eventually quit assigning him to work details. He just sat in our cell trying to think of a way to con someone out of their money. I think he's going stir-crazy. You want to keep your distance from him. I, on the other hand, liked the work details. Got my mind off things and got me outside. Hey, you had dinner? I get to eat all my meals at the Ritz Hotel Bistro free of charge. I'm telling you, this ball-playing is wonderful."

Katy reported her interview with Daniel Poul to her boss and got the keys to his Studebaker for the trip to the Tucker Farm the next day. She was supposed to meet with the prison officials at one and had an interview scheduled with Gleason immediately following. She was scared. Women didn't go by themselves to places like the Tucker Farm. Then it hit her, she ought to take someone—someone big, someone like Big Bear Radisson. That evening she took the Studebaker to his pool-hall, but was told he was in training and was living at the Ritz Hotel, so she went back to town and called his room from the bistro bar.

In a few minutes the biggest man in town lowered his head as he got off the elevator and walked toward the bar at one end of the dining area.

He held out a massive paw. "You Miss Katy Hamelin?"

"I am."

"I'm Bear Radisson, Miss Hamelin."

Katy slipped from her bar stool and said, "Mr. Radisson, let's go to a table."

At the table, Faye ordered a rum and coke and waited for her king-sized guest to order.

"I'll have unsweetened iced tea. Leave off the lemon, please." Bear looked at the woman from Mr. Jellico's office. "I don't drink. Besides, I'm in training."

"Mr. Radisson, have you ever seen this man?" She produced a picture of Evan Bonds she had cut from a Wind Springs High School yearbook.

"No. I don't think so. Who is he?"

"He's the man we think killed Raylene and my husband."

"And you think he might have come to my pool hall?"

"It was a long shot. No one's seen him since the first trial. He was the one who kidnapped Faye and held her for ransom in the Ghent

Bank Building. I was hoping he'd been in your place sometime during that period. But I guess he's left the country. We've checked the bus station and they don't have a record of him buying a ticket. His car was found with a half tank of gas. Mr. Jellico thinks he ran out of money and got a ride somewhere when his finances wouldn't let him replace the gasoline."

"No. I haven't seen him. But I've been here a week. I got my little brother minding the pool hall while I sharpen my ball skills."

"Do you think we'll win the game?"

"Hard to say. We're a lot better than we were, but these other guys are almost professional. If we don't win, we've decided to bundle them up in toe sacks and ship them back east in a cattle truck."

"Now, is that any way to show southern hospitality?"

"Ma'am, these men are damn Yankees."

"I see. Well, I have one more question. No, make that two questions."

"Shoot."

"Are you allowed to take a day off from your training?"

"With a reasonable excuse. And number two?"

"Would you accompany me tomorrow to the Tucker Farm? I have to interview Evan Bonds' brother and I'm scared. I've never been to a prison before."

"I'd be happy to. Would we be riding a bus?"

"No. I have Mr. Jellico's Studebaker."

"Okay, but I can't drive."

"You don't know how?"

"No. The front seat won't move far enough back from the steering wheel. I won't be able to get in on the driver's side."

"You might be surprised. Mr. Jellico is not as tall, but he's much bigger around the waist and he gets in just fine."

"Whatever. Where do you want to meet me and what time?"

"Mr. Radisson—may I call you Bear?"

"Only if I can call you Kate."

"Bear, my friends call me Katy."

"Has anyone ever called you Kate?"

"No, I don't think so."

"Good, 'cause I'm not like any man you've ever met."

"Okay, Bear, I'll pick you up here tomorrow morning at six. Is that too early?"

"Certainly not. Coach has us at the ball field warming up when daylight breaks and, except for our meals, we don't get back till dark. I'll be ready."

The next morning Bear looked at the driver's side of Jellico's Studebaker. He'd been right. There was no way he'd be able to get his six-foot-seven, three-hundred pounds in there. He was going to have a hard enough time getting in the passenger side where there wasn't a steering wheel.

Katy watched in amusement for a moment as Bear tried a foot and a leg first, then pulled them out and tried to back in. At one point he sat in the seat, but couldn't get his left leg through the gap left in front of the seat.

Katy reached over and grabbed his knee, giving it a hefty tug and pulling it past the door jamb. His foot was still outside. "Bear, have you thought of moving the seat back as far as it'll go?"

"No. I thought it was already as far back as it would go. But now I can't reach the lever."

Katy reached under his seat, getting her blouse caught on the gear selector knob. After breaking free and losing the top two buttons, she decided to reach under the driver's seat to find out just where that lever might be, thinking it would be in the same location on the passenger's seat. She found it and pulled it to the left. Her seat slid back until it touched the back seat, making it so far from the steering wheel that the tips of her toes were a foot shy of the pedals. Her hands couldn't reach the steering wheel until she scooted to the front of the seat.

Bear laughed. "At least we now know how Mr. Jellico gets in. Do you think he's had the passenger seat fixed the same way?"

"It doesn't matter. I'm going to come around there and pry you loose. You can drive, that is, if your feet will reach the pedals. This is like trying to drive from the back seat." Katy crawled out and circled the car. She saw several people staring out the windows of the restaurant when she sailed by. "Bear, how did you get your leg in there?"

"While you were on the floorboard looking for the seat lever I thought I'd better figure something out or you'd be leaving me behind. I

104

took off my shoe, gritted my teeth, and banged my chin with my kneecap."

"Here, let me help you out. There's now plenty of room on the other side. Do you think you could stretch that leg over the center console?"

"Maybe, if you were over there to pull."

Katy ran back to the driver's side. On the way, she noticed lots more people were now at the window. "Okay, you leave that other leg outside on the right. I'm going to pull this one over here to my side."

"Lady, my legs don't work that way."

Katy didn't listen. She grabbed his foot and the cuff to his pants and, putting her two feet against the console and her backside on the floorboard, she leaned back and pulled. His foot moved to the top of the console. She tried again, yanking with all of her might. This time she heard two loud noises: Bear Radisson screaming for mercy and his pants ripping.

"Oh, Bear, I'm so sorry. Listen, you stay right here. I'm going inside to get us a cup of coffee. This has wore me out."

"Damnit, Kate. You're one scatter-brained broad. Let loose of my leg and I'll get out on my own."

Katy jumped out of the driver's side and ran around the car one more time. When she got to the passenger side, six or eight people stood there trying to get a closer glimpse of what was going on inside the car.

Harriet said, "Katy, do you have him where you want him yet?"

Not much was said for the first hundred miles. Big Bear Radisson now wore a second pair of pants and he drove. Harriet had fixed Katy's blouse with safety pins she'd found in the concierge's station. Then they were off. Katy had time to purchase two cups of coffee and two breakfast rolls, but Bear said he didn't like sweets. He did, however, take the coffee.

"Bear, if you don't eat sweets, and I haven't noticed you eating snacks between meals, how did you get to be so big?"

"I'm not fat. I'm just big. It's potatoes. My father's a farmer. His big crop is potatoes and my mother knows how to fix them a hundred different ways. We're all big."

"Are you going to be all right? I mean, I didn't hurt anything permanent, did I?"

"I don't know. I'll tell you this, though. I have a new regard for people who dance ballet."

"You ever thought about losing weight?"

"Yeah. And shrinking down to a normal height. And cutting off my toes so I wouldn't have to wear special-order shoes."

"Now you're just being ridiculous. I didn't mean to hurt you."

"The last woman who hurt me tore my heart apart. Hell, all you did was start a little lower. I'll be okay, but if I ever get married and you see some woman heading your way with a stick, you should probably run."

"Are you aware a man from the *Marsden County Meteor* took your picture?"

"No. Really?"

"Yes. I think it's going to be in the paper. He stood behind the car. He got your left foot extending from the driver's side and most of your right leg and foot sticking out from the passenger's side."

"Well, where were you?"

"I had to snap the picture. He was laughing so hard he couldn't hold the camera steady."

Nothing more was said until they pulled up to the front gate of the main Arkansas State Prison called the Tucker Farm. They were given visitor's passes and ushered into a secure area before being admitted into the administration building. To the warden Katy handed the subpoena Judge McAdams had signed telling him to produce the inmate known as Gleason Bonds to the Marsden County Jail on Wednesday of the following week. The county would provide a secure cell for his incarceration while away from the Tucker Farm. The prison could come and get him after his testimony was complete or the county would provide separate quarters for any correctional deputy who might wish to stay for the duration. The judge anticipated his complete testimony to take two days.

The warden looked over the papers, stamped the time and date, and put them in a filling tray. "You want to interview Mr. Bonds now, I suppose."

"Yes, sir."

"Guards, bring Mr. Bonds to the visitation room. Miss Hamelin, you and Mr. Radisson will be escorted by a guard to the interview. We do not consider Mr. Bonds dangerous. But you will not be allowed any physical contact. You may not give him anything, receive anything from him, or shake his hand. You will sit at a table separated from him by a thick mesh wire. A security guard will be in the room at all times. Do both of you understand this?"

Both nodded in agreement.

Bear asked, "Can we add money to his account for cigarettes and snacks?"

"Up to twenty dollars each month."

Katy handed the warden two crisp bills and they followed a guard to the visitation area. When Gleason arrived he looked around, but the only visitors were Katy and Bear. He walked over to his side of the wire and said, "You want to see me? I thought my brother, Evan, had come."

Katy and Bear moved to chairs opposite Gleason. Katy looked Gleason straight in the eye. "No, Mr. Bonds, but it's Evan we've come about. He's missing. Your father hasn't seen Evan in three months. He's worried."

"And he wouldn't come and ask me himself?"

"Your father didn't send us. Evan robbed a woman's apartment in Dancing Deer three months ago and we think he's left for Mexico. Do you have any information that might help us find him?"

"No, but he should've come by here before he lit out like that. He owes me money."

"Mr. Bonds, we put twenty dollars in your account. Will that help?"

"Yeah. But Evan owes me more than that. He was going to start depositing twenty dollars every month."

"Our money was supplied by Daniel Poul. He said he'd start sending you money as he could. I think he's now got a job."

"Well, it's about time. He owes me a ton of money as well."

"Mr. Bonds, how do you make your money while in here?"

"I gamble."

"I see. And the money Evan owes you was gambling winnings as well?"

"No. That was a financial investment."

"Did it involve the ten thousand dollars Raylene Carlisle had?"

"Uh . . . I don't know anything about that."

"Really, Mr. Bonds. Evan told several people how you gave him the information about Raylene's money. He said he was planning on spending your share first. That was right after the burglary. If you could help us find him, we might be able to have him spend his time right here with you. You were close to your younger brother, weren't you?"

"Yeah. But I won't rat on him."

"If you were just to confirm that you were the one to supply him with the information of Raylene's money, whether he stole it or not, I might arrange for you to receive enough money to keep you in cigarettes and snacks for the next two years."

"Yeah, I'll take that deal."

"You'd have to tell a judge who's trying a man accused of doing the same crime."

"Evan had help?"

"We don't know that."

"It doesn't matter. Yeah, I'll tell the judge. When will you start putting money in my account?"

"We put in twenty dollars today and we'll start the first Friday after your testimony and again on the last day of every month for two years."

"When will I get to talk with the judge?"

"Next week."

"Sounds good to me. You got me a bus ticket?"

"No, the warden is going to deliver you. Good day, Mr. Bonds."

On the way back to Dancing Deer, Katy was in good spirits and suggested they stop for a late lunch. Mr. Jellico had given her money for their meal and she felt like having seafood. Bear said there were mighty few restaurants in Arkansas that sold seafood, but if she liked catfish there were plenty of restaurants selling that.

"I have to say, Kate. You impressed me with your ability to interrogate. No more the crazy broad routine. No, you were strictly professional, and skilled."

"So now you think the episode this morning was an act to put you off your guard."

"No, I think it was a calculated exercise to rip my pants off."

"Mr. Bear Radisson, you are too funny."

CHAPTER 21 – THE CASE FOR THE PROSECUTION

The courtroom was noisy, as independent conversations saturated the room. By the door stood Rafe or Ralph Johnson, a nephew of the defendant and one of the twin brothers who served as the Marsden County deputy sheriffs. Beyond this first legal boundary were two sections of seating separated by a wide aisle. Visitors and interested citizens, who would not be called as witnesses, sat in the two sections. Chattering proliferated in their territory which was separated from the official court proceedings by a waist-high railing. Beyond the railing, on the left the defendant Marsden County Sheriff Sherman Shodtoe and his attorney Michael Jellico sat at a clean table. On the right the prosecutor sat at a second table, this one littered with folders, paper memos, and the dregs of a tattered briefcase. The prosecutor's name was Emmett Irving, the District Attorney for Marsden County. To the right of the prosecutor's table and somewhat elevated against the wall, two rows of chairs held the jury with six alternates off to one side. Closer still sat the bailiff to the left, the court reporter in the center, and a vacant chair for witnesses to the right of the court reporter. All the way to the front, two steps up from the floor and surrounded by a four-foot railing stood a massive narrow bench. Behind this bench the judge presided.

"All stand for the Honorable Judge Murphy McAdams, Marsden County judge for the state of Arkansas."

The judge entered, told everyone to be seated, and sat down himself. From his chair he announced the legal description of the case being tried and asked if the prosecution was ready. After receiving an affirmative reply, he asked the defense if they were ready.

Jellico said "Yes. Your Honor."

Judge McAdams told Mr. Irving he could proceed.

Emmett had made this same speech to different jurors just months before. Only the name of the accused had changed. For that first trial, for the murder of Raylene Carlisle and Galen Hamelin, the defendant had been Bill Potter. Emmett failed miserably to convince anyone Bill was guilty. Jellico, for the defense, painted a picture of the sheriff as the one who should have been charged. As Jellico's evidence grew, damning the sheriff, Emmett's case started easing to the toilet. Finally, Emmett had to tell the judge that the State no longer thought Bill Potter guilty of the crime and wanted to cease his prosecution.

Now Emmett stood before a different set of jurors, making a similar speech. He told them what the State thought the sheriff did, listed the evidence in an abbreviated form, and said that under the weight of the evidence he was prepared to present, the good people of the State of Arkansas, the same ones this jury of twelve represents, would have no choice but to convict.

Going back to his seat, he inwardly thanked Jellico for piling up the evidence for him. However, this Mr. Jellico, who Emmett had earlier considered an inconsequential lawyer of less-than-adequate talents, was again his adversary. A bit more respected this time. A bit more polished in his briefs. A more formidable opponent than Emmett Irving had wanted. But it was he who had accumulated the evidence, pointed the damning finger, and it was Jellico who had built the case against the sheriff. District Attorney Emmett Irving would use all of Jellico's work plus one witness and two articles of evidence he'd added himself. One very important witness. He would have his retaliation for so blatantly losing the first go 'round.

Jellico wore a new suit perfectly hand-tailored to fit his massive frame. He'd put his fee from the first case back into his practice and into his personal appearance. He thought if you wanted to be a successful lawyer, you needed to make that appearance. He'd hired a secretary to modernize his office, to schedule his appointments, to categorize his expenses, to bill his customers, and to relieve him of anything that kept him from putting his total concentration toward the case at hand. This new administrative assistant had settled in with such skill and level of organization, Jellico wondered how he had ever gotten along without her. He considered the four of them a formidable force. One Emmett Irving would soon be reeling from. By the four, of course, he meant himself, his new assistant, his receptionist, and Katy Hamelin, his detective at large.

Jellico stood up and walked briskly to the jury box. "Ladies and gentlemen of the jury, this is it. You are about to participate in one of the great building blocks our forefathers founded this country on. A right to trial by a jury of one's peers. Now some people might shirk their duty as an annoyance or they might fear retaliation by an interested party. But I'm here to tell you that the wheels of justice transport everyone, whether rich or poor, white or black, of good moral substance or the lowest of knaves, to freedom for the innocent and incarceration or death for the guilty. Do not take this civic responsibility too lightly.

"For you to find Sheriff Sherman Shodtoe guilty of either murder, you cannot have any reservations. You have to be completely convinced, beyond the shadow of a'doubt, of his guilt. I don't mean guilty of the petty little things all civil servants are tempted with— falsifying traffic tickets or stealing money from the petty cash fund. No. You have to look at the evidence given by Mr. Irving and come to the conclusion, based on that evidence, that this man perpetrated our state's most heinous offense—murder." Jellico spoke the word slowly rolling the "r" in a deep resonating voice. Several women shivered and hair raised on the necks of men.

"But if I cast doubt on his guilt; if I give you evidence that someone else committed the crime; if I inform you about a sequence of events leading up to the crime, with the sheriff as only an onlooker, with no actual participation; then I will have given you sufficient reason to doubt his guilt, and you have no choice, no choice . . ." Jellico made eye contact with several jurors ". . . other than to find Sheriff Sherman Shodtoe not guilty."

One after another of Jellico's defense witnesses in the first trial were now called as witnesses for the prosecution. There was Galen's wife, Katy Hamelin, now working for the defense, who testified that although she told several people—including the police—about her husband's ties with organized crime in Chicago, she told only the defendant they were running from the Canneli brothers.

There was Beatrice Bentback, the switchboard operator at the telephone exchange, who testified about two telephone calls from the sheriff's apartment to Chicago, and one from Chicago to his apartment. She also affirmed a new piece of evidence provided by the telephone company, stating that the first call placed from the sheriff's apartment went to the Canneli Brothers Import and Export Company, the second call was to the sheriff's apartment from Edward Canneli's residence, and the third from the sheriff's apartment again to the Canneli Brothers Import and Export Company.

There was Charles Jimmerson, the acting manager at the bank during Bill's absence, who testified that Sheriff Shodtoe received an anonymous bank wire from Chicago for five thousand dollars four days after Mr. Hamelin's funeral. Bank examiners in Chicago provided another piece of evidence, an affidavit stating the bank wire came from the Canneli Brothers Import and Export Company's general account.

The second day, the prosecution brought forth the coroner. He testified about the methods by which the two victims were murdered and about Sheriff Shodtoe's house slipper with a blood stain matching Galen Hamelin's blood type. He also presented five twenty-dollar bills having Hamelin's and Bill Potter's fingerprints. The shoes and money were found with a search warrant of the sheriff's apartment, office, and squad car.

In the afternoon of the second day, the prosecution swore in Officer Raymond Henderson, Sheriff Shodtoe's cousin. Emmett established Raymond's name for the record and his relationship to the defendant. He then grilled him on the particularities of the case being tried.

"Officer Henderson . . ."

"I'm just Raymond Henderson. I've resigned my position as police officer for the City of Dancing Deer."

"Yes, well, would you please tell the court your duties when you were employed by the City of Dancing Deer as a police officer."

"Certainly. Besides patrolling the streets with Officer McRae, I was responsible for the security of the items in the evidence room."

"Did the defendant ever ask you to steal anything from the evidence room?"

"Yes. A couple of days before the murder of Galen Hamelin, he asked me for a piece that could not be identified."

"And what did he mean by 'piece' and 'could not be identified.'"

Jellico jumped from his chair. "Objection, Your Honor. Calls for speculation."

Emmett Irving said, "Your Honor, these are normal terms of speech used by the military and law enforcement. They are not ambiguous, but also may not be in the vernacular of an individual unacquainted with the jargon of either of these two agencies. Certainly Mr. Henderson, as a career police officer, can speak with authority on the attributes of either of these two terms."

"I agree, Mr. Irving. Overruled."

"Exception."

"So noted. Answer the question, Mr. Henderson."

"A 'piece,' in the military, is the firearm for which an individual is responsible. It can be an M1 rifle, an M1 carbine, a grenade launcher, a howitzer, and so on. To a police officer it is a handgun, either a revolver or an automatic. 'Could not be identified' means with its serial number filed off."

"Thank you, Mr. Henderson. Did you provide the sheriff with such a piece?"

"Yes."

"From the evidence room?"

"Yes."

"Your Honor, the prosecution wants entered into the record Exhibit 4. Now, Mr. Henderson, is this the piece?"

"Yes."

"What did he do with the gun when you delivered it to him?"

"He put it in his pocket and said 'Thank you.'"

"And, Mr. Henderson, did you ever see the gun again?"

"Early on the morning of the day after Mr. Hamelin's murder, he came by my house and told me to use a steel brush on the inside of the barrel and to plant it in Bill Potter's car."

"And you did that?"

"Yes."

"Mr. Henderson, did the defendant ask you to further implicate Mr. Potter in the murder of Raylene Carlisle or Galen Hamelin?"

"Yes. During our search of Mr. Potter's house and automobile. We were supposed to look for, among other things, a right shoe with blood stains. We confiscated a right shoe from every pair in Mr. Potter's closet. None of them contained any blood stains, so Sherman . . . "

"The defendant?"

"Yes . . . Sherman . . . I mean Mr. Shodtoe told me to smear one droplet of blood on the stitching of the upper part of the sole. He said if I used a tiny amount it would not be enough for the coroner to type and, although it would not be Mr. Hamelin's blood, the implication would be there and it could not be said that it wasn't."

"And you did this?"

"Yes. Then I told Chief Wainwright that I thought the coroner's office returned the shoes too quickly. I told him I thought they should recheck them with a magnifying glass. After this second effort, they found the smear I had put on the shoe."

"Mr. Henderson, did you receive any money from the defendant for your help in implicating Mr. Potter?"

"Yes. I received an envelope with five hundred dollars."

"Your witness, counselor." District Attorney Emmett Irving strode confidently back to his chair at the prosecution table.

Jellico slowly stood. "Mr. Henderson, did Sheriff Shodtoe, the defendant, kill either Raylene Carlisle or Galen Hamelin?"

"No."

"You're absolutely certain?"

"Positive."

"Your Honor, I have no further questions for this witness at this time. However, I would like to ask him additional questions later in the trial after more evidence has been introduced."

"Mr. Irving?"

"The State has no problem with that, Your Honor."

"Your next witness, Mr. Irving?"

"Your Honor, the State rests."

"In that case, this court is adjourned. We will reconvene tomorrow morning at nine." The judge slammed down his gavel and walked from the court.

CHAPTER 22 – A BEAR IN THE WOODS

Bear needed to check on his business. He knew his brother would do his best, but he was no business man. Bear skipped the evening meal and walked into Snockered about eight in the evening. Curfew was at nine so he had one hour before he had to be back at the hotel.

When Bear opened the door, well-wishers slapped him on his back or yelled from across the room. Some clapped, some whistled, and some paid little attention. His place was packed.

Bear walked up to his kid brother behind the bar. "Sampson, how's it going? You making enough to pay the bills?"

"Don't know. I ain't paid no bills yet. All I do is rent out this snooker table, make change for the eight-ball tables and juke box, and pour drinks. Man, I thought you had an easy job."

"What do you mean you ain't paid no bills yet?"

"Yeah, Mom and Dad come by every morning. I put everything in a sack. I keep a hundred dollars in ones and change in the till and stuff everything else in the sack. Mom goes through the sack, makes out the deposit, and sends Dad to the bank. He makes the deposit and brings back rolls of change. The trucks come every other day. Mom has their last bill payment under the money tray in the till. We even got Sally cleaning tables and hauling out trash. Bear, how'd you get everything done by yourself? It takes all of us now you're gone."

"I worked my tail off, that's how. So there been anything interesting happen?"

"One nice-looking lady came in saying she was your friend and wanted to learn how to shoot pool."

"What did she look like. Did she give you her name. Was it Kate Hamelin?"

"No, it wasn't Miss Hamelin. She didn't say who she was, but she did create quite a stir. She had short brown hair and a real good-looking figure. Lots of men offered to show her how to play pool, but

117

she said you told her to ask me. Hell, Bear, I'm no pool player. Every time I told her something, one of the guys said no that wasn't right and proceeded to give her better instructions. I think she started picking it up though. Must've been five men around the table correcting everything I said. Once she went to the juke box, but before she could get her money out two men were there begging to pay for her."

"So you don't know who she was, but the men fell over themselves to be of assistance."

"Pretty much." Sampson took a rag and wiped away a wet circle on the bar. "Say, I'll bet that deputy knows who she is. I'll ask him tonight and get back to you."

"Okay, I got to go. When this is over I'll make everything right with you."

"Think maybe you might expand? I could run a similar joint in Skunk Hollow."

"Now that's an idea. We'll talk about it. I gotta go. See you, Sampson. Keep up the good work and close down for the game. I want everybody there."

"You got it, bro."

Katy was scheduled to be on the witness stand for the second time, in the afternoon. This time for the defense. She decided to get her hair done in case there was someone in the audience she needed to impress.

"Gena, you got time to do my nails?"

"Sure, honey."

"So, Gena, what do you think about a woman dating a younger man?"

"I think its great if you can get away with it. You got a younger man in mind?"

"No. I was just thinking in general. I haven't found anyone I'm interested in that's my age so thought I might look around. Who might be good prospects?"

"I think Daniel Poul is good-looking. And there are those Johnson boys and three men in the McKesson family. In the forty age bracket though, the pickings are mighty slim. You got a lot more to choose from with the men in their thirties."

"That's what I was thinking. But Daniel Poul still looks like a young man. If I was to date someone younger than myself, he'd still have to look like a man capable of taking care of his lady. I don't want no boys."

"Katy, honey, let me think on it." Three other women listening in thought they might think on it as well.

Katy decided to call Harriet. She wanted to get herself invited to some of the parties to which the ball players were being invited. The town was doing everything it could for its boys. Gena gave them free haircuts. Of course they could go to Ossie's and there they would get a free haircut and also a free shoeshine. Friday and Saturday nights were the only nights they didn't have to be in their rooms by nine, so the town planned dances and small parties,

"Harriet, have you got a minute?"

"Sure, what do you need?"

"I need someone to talk to. Now that Faye is in New York City, I'm by myself again and bored to death. I was wondering if you needed someone to run errands. I can keep notes, mend uniforms, bring water. You name it."

"I think that would be great. Why don't you show up tomorrow in our strategy room and we'll see. It's at the Ritz, first room down the hall from the bistro. Be there at seven."

"Okay, today we're going to work on position. You can't stake out an area of the playing field and think that's your only area of work. You also have to back up other players. When the play is going to be at third, someone has to be shy and someone has to be long. The runner is heading to the bag, so that's where the play needs to be made, but an errant throw that gets away will not only allow him to arrive safely, but might also allow him to continue home. The catcher can't leave the plate, so the pitcher has to come over and back up third with short in front. Now short, you want to be on a direct line between where the ball will be thrown and the bag. If it's wide, you catch the ball. If the runner is going to make the bag safely, you catch the ball, but if the ball is bearing down on you and there's a chance of getting the out, step out of the way and let the third baseman make the play. Also, if there's a runner advancing to second, short, you have to decide which is the right play. Sometimes you'll have an easier out by grabbing the ball and flipping to second.

"Okay. Now, second, the right fielder might realize the better play is at your base, especially if he has to go deep so you get on his side of the bag. You don't want the runner interfering with your ability to catch the ball, so you catch the ball on the fielder's side of the bag and swipe backwards with the ball held tight in the pocket. If no runner is going to third, you're the shy one. You go into shallow right, let short cover the bag and either the pitcher or third back him up. If there's a possibility he'll be heading on to third then, third, you have to stay at your base and the pitcher backs up the play at second.

"Listen up. You can't impede the runner. If he has to run over you because you're in the base path, he'll be awarded another base."

"Fielders, you got to be alert. When men are on base you got to be moving your feet when the pitcher releases the ball. You don't want a ball hit to you and you find out your feet are frozen to the ground. Always think several scenarios ahead. For instance think, 'If it's hit to me shallow, where do I throw it. If it's hit to me deep, where do I throw it. If I have to run it down, where do I throw it.' Get rid of it quickly and throw it to the right place. Think ahead. Play smart. The Hotshots are semi-pro. They won't be making mistakes and neither can we."

Katy was amazed at how the men paid attention to a woman telling them how to play baseball. They listened, cocked their heads, and often wrote something in their playbook.

"Catch, who do you back up?"

David Blaine said, "First, if the play is at first and if there isn't anyone on third or running from second. No other backups"

"That's right. First, where do you play when a runner is coming home and the throw comes from right field?"

Bear said, "I play shy for home, catching any errant throw or any good throw if there's a better play. I'm to use my own judgment, understanding an out at home saves a run."

"Good. That's all for now. We'll break for lunch. Leave your playbooks. We'll be back to talk about hitting strategy after lunch, and then at three I want everyone on the field. We'll take batting practice.

I'm going to show you how you can speed up your swing. This evening we'll finish by practicing the three different kinds of slides, and then, as always, you'll take ten laps around the park."

As they walked down the hall to the restaurant Katy said, "Harriet how did you learn so much about baseball?"

"All my brothers played and my father was a minor league manager. My entire adolescence was spent idolizing someone who breathed baseball. When I got old enough to date, my father was so protective I had to invent ways to meet boys. I found he would let me attend baseball games, so I became the only female member of the Boston Royal Rooters. They walked to the ball park in one big group from 'Nuff Said' McGreevy's 3rd Base Saloon. I stepped into the rabble a block or so from the stadium, and when they went through the turnstiles I slid under. It was so much fun. And I learned a lot about baseball, mostly out of self defense. I can't hit the ball, but I know a good swing when I see it—and strategy. We argued strategy between batters and got more in depth between innings."

"Well, I'm impressed."

"Are you having fun, Katy?"

"It's good to have someone to talk to. Say, does Bill give you any static?"

"No, he's just like one of the boys. I don't cut him any slack. Have you seen how the men have gotten their stamina back? I've heard several men say they've lost weight."

"You'd be surprised how important a good diet and plenty of sleep is."

"No, Katy, I wouldn't. I was the one who set up the regimen and told Andre what to prepare for their meals. I was really talking about you. I think you ought to move into the Ritz, eat with the team, and observe curfew."

"Do you allow reading in bed?"

CHAPTER 23 – JELLICO FOR THE DEFENSE

"May it please the court, the defense wishes to call Daniel Poul to the witness stand."

Rafe, or maybe Ralph, headed to where the witnesses were stashed and quickly led in Daniel carrying his playbook.

Daniel spent a few moments getting his name entered into the court records and being sworn in. With this accomplished, Jellico walked forward from the defense table and asked, "Is it true, Mr. Poul, that you have recently been released on parole from the Tucker Farm?"

"Three months ago."

"Please tell the court the circumstances resulting in your incarceration at the Tucker Farm."

"I snuck into my neighbor's house and stole her savings while her relatives were lowering her into the ground. When I left her house a neighbor saw me."

"What did you do with the pilfered money, Mr. Poul?"

"I gave it to Raylene to keep for me. She put it in a shoebox."

"And was it recovered by the police?"

"No. I was charged with stealing an undetermined amount of money and a watch worth more than a hundred dollars. Mr. Irving offered me a deal for a guilty plea. I was sentenced to fifteen years."

"During your stint at the Tucker Farm, did you tell anyone about the money?"

"No."

"Did Miss Carlisle come to visit you?"

"Yes. For several years she came regularly. Each time she tried to talk me into giving the money back, but I was stubborn. She eventually quit coming, just writing. That lasted for a year or two. But she always said the same thing—that I should give the ten thousand dollars back."

"What did you do with those letters, Mr. Poul?"

"I gave them to your detective, Katy Hamelin."

123

Jellico went to the defense table, picked up a cellophane sack, and returned to the witness stand. "Mr. Poul, are these those letters?"

"Yes, sir."

"The defense wants to introduce into evidence items D five, Your Honor."

"Mr. Poul, where did you keep these letters?"

"In a box on top of my locker."

"Locked?"

"No, sir. We don't have locks within our cells."

"Now, Mr. Poul, would you tell the court the name of your cellmate for the two months prior to Miss Carlisle's murder."

"Gleason Bonds."

"Did Mr. Bonds have access to your letters?"

"Yes. I worked on outside details when I could, but Gleason always had an excuse and stayed in our cell. Since they weren't locked up or anything, he could have gone through my things any number of times and if he did he would have found the letters."

Emmett Irving said, "I object, Your Honor. Calls for speculation."

"Sustained. Rephrase your question, Mr. Jellico."

"Mr. Poul, were your letters kept in a secure place?"

"No."

"Did Mr. Bonds work on details with you?"

"No."

"Thank you, Mr. Poul. Your witness, Mr. Irving."

"I have no questions."

"The defense calls Katy Hamelin to the stand."

"Miss Hamelin, you're still under oath from your previous testimony. Do you understand this?"

"Yes."

"It's my understanding that your sister was kidnapped and held for ransom during the earlier trial when Mr. Bill Potter was accused."

Emmett Irving was out of his chair. "Your Honor. The defense is testifying for the witness. And the state has no record of Miss Hamelin's sister swearing out a report saying she was kidnapped. Mr.

Jellico needs to produce this sister. Any information Miss Hamelin could give would only be hearsay."

"Mr. Jellico?"

"Your Honor. Miss Hamelin's sister left for New York City with Chief of Police, W.W. Wainwright soon after Bill Potter's trial was terminated. She has not yet returned."

"I'm sorry, Mr. Jellico, unless you can corroborate the allegation, any reference to an abduction is out. Continue, Mr. Jellico."

"Uh . . . Miss Hamelin, were you in court when your sister appeared?"

"Yes."

"What did she look like and what did she say?"

"She was barefoot, her clothes were disheveled, her hair was sticking out in all directions, and she was dirty. She said she had been abducted and held for ransom three blocks from here. She wanted to know what her taxes were for if they were not used for protecting citizens. She criticized Chief Wainwright for not finding her and Bill Potter for not paying her ransom. She also compared our police officers to the Keystone Cops."

"Thank you, Miss Hamelin. Your witness."

"No questions."

Judge McAdams said, "This court will break for lunch. We will reconvene at one p.m."

Jellico walked out of the courtroom shaking his head. Katy came along and matched Jellico's strides. "Let me take you to lunch."

"Thank you, Katy. Have you heard from your sister?"

"No, I haven't."

"It probably wouldn't matter anyway. There's no way we can prove her abductor was Evan Bonds. I've got two more witnesses. Gleason and Sheriff Shodtoe. Then we'll see if the jury bought into our hypothesis. I did a much better job with Bill. The sheriff might fry for something he didn't do and for a poor performance by his defense council."

"I have all the faith in the world in you, Jellico. You'll find a way."

That afternoon Jellico called Gleason Bonds to the stand. "Mr. Bonds, were you the cellmate of Daniel Poul at the Tucker Farm?"

"I was for January and February of this year."

"Have you had any visitors, Mr. Bonds?"

"You mean besides your two detectives?"

"Yes, Mr. Bonds—excluding those."

"Only my brother, Evan. Everyone else thinks I'm not worth their time."

"I see. Mr. Bonds, what kind of car does your brother drive?"

"Dad gave him a green Plymouth."

"Mr. Bonds, during those months you shared a cell with Daniel Poul, did you ever have occasion to check out his possessions?"

"Yeah. He owed me money and I thought he might be holding out."

"Did you find any money?"

"No. Just some letters that said this woman was holding his money for him till he got out."

"Did you communicate this to your brother on one of his visits?"

"Yeah. I told him to ask the woman if she would use some of that money to pay off his debts."

"Did he do that?"

"I don't know, he never came back. I haven't seen him or any of my money."

"Thank you, Mr. Bonds. Your witness, counselor."

"Mr. Bonds, were you the only cellmate Mr. Poul had?"

"No. He'd been in for seven years. I landed in prison in January of this year."

"Is it a common practice to steal another man's cigarettes when he's out on a work detail?"

"Yeah. Happens all the time."

"And during a ransacking they would have run across his letters?"

"Yeah."

"So there are any number of people who might know about this money?"

"Yeah."

"Thank you, Mr. Bonds. Just a minute, Mr. Bonds. Did the defense pay you anything for your testimony?"

"Cigarette and snack money for two years."

"Thank you, Mr. Bonds, that will be all."

"Next witness, Mr. Jellico."

"Mr. Sherman Shodtoe, Your Honor."

"Very well. Mr. Shodtoe would you take the stand and tell us your name for the record."

"Sherman Stanley Shodtoe."

"Raise your right hand, Mr. Shodtoe. Do you swear to tell the truth, the whole truth, and nothing but the truth, so help you God?"

There was snickering throughout the courtroom as the sheriff said, "I do."

"Sheriff, is your apartment on the third floor of an apartment building directly across the street from Miss Carlisle's?"

"Yes."

"What were you doing on the night Miss Carlisle was murdered?"

"I enjoy star-gazing. I have a telescope to look at the stars. On Friday nights Faye Spencer works late and walks home from the paper some time between ten and midnight. Besides star-gazing, I keep a watch for her."

"So you were in your bedroom with the window open looking for Miss Spencer with your telescope?"

"Yes, sir."

"Did you see anything unusual?"

"At nine-thirty Bill Potter drove up and parked in front of the next apartment over. Normally he parks a block or so away and sneaks in the back to Miss Carlisle's apartment."

"Objection. Calls for speculation."

"Sustained. Mr. Shodtoe, you have no way of knowing Mr. Potter was going specifically to Miss Carlisle's apartment. So that portion of your answer is stricken from your testimony. Answer what you know, not what you surmise. Continue, Mr. Jellico."

"Thank you, Your Honor. Mr. Shodtoe. How long was Mr. Potter in the apartment building across the street?"

"Twenty minutes."

"Did you see Miss Carlisle?"

"Yes. She waved to him from the building's front door as he drove off."

"And what happened next?"

"A green Plymouth pulled away from the curb and followed Potter's Packard."

"Had Miss Spencer arrived home by this time?"

"No, she arrived an hour later. Normally, she arrives between ten and midnight. This time it was around eleven."

"What happened next?"

"She went inside. The green Plymouth had arrived thirty minutes earlier and parked in front of the building next door. Using the telescope, I got his license plate number. A man got out of the car and went into Miss Carlisle's apartment building.

Right behind Miss Spencer another man came walking down the sidewalk. He walked up to the front door of Miss Carlisle's apartment building and tried the front door, but it was now locked. He hid in the bushes by the front door. I think he . . . ."

"Mr. Shodtoe, stick to what you know."

"Yes, sir, Mr. Jellico."

"And what happened next?"

"Thirty more minutes passed and the man from the green Plymouth came out the front door. He saw the man in the bushes and walked over to where the man crouched. They must've had words because the man in the bushes decked the man from the green Plymouth, knocking him to the ground.

"He got up, ran into the apartment building using a key to get in, and locked the door behind him. The man in the bushes ran to the front door but was too late. It was locked. He tried to climb a drainpipe, fell, and then walked around to the back of the building. He came back to the front when the man from the green Plymouth came out the front door carrying a pillow. He walked up close to the man from the bushes and shot him through the pillow. He then got in the green Plymouth and drove off."

"So, Sheriff Shodtoe, what did you do?"

"I went downstairs . . . ."

"In your slippers?"

"Yeah, in my slippers. I reached the body. The wind whistled. It was cold. No one was out. I went through the dead man's clothes, took five twenty dollar bills, and went to call the police."

"Did you tell the police who you were?"

"No. Just there was a man dead and his location. I hung up and waited to watch their investigation from my bedroom window."

"And the next day?"

"Early that morning, I went to my cousin Raymond Henderson's house. I handed him the gun he had given me and told him to plant it in Potter's car. Two days prior, on the fifteenth, I called the Canneli Brothers Import and Export Company in Chicago and asked the manager if they had a contract out on Galen Hamelin. A scratchy voice took my number. The next day someone from the company called me back and told me I could earn five thousand for killing Galen Hamelin. I was given another number to call when it had been done. I waited a couple of days and called. I also sent a copy of our newspaper when they listed the funeral in the obituary section. They sent me the money and I gave five hundred to Raymond for handling the gun."

"So, Sheriff Shodtoe, you didn't kill Raylene Carlisle or Galen Hamelin?"

"No. Evan Bonds did—the driver of the green Plymouth."

Emmett raised his hand. "Your Honor. The defense needs to produce this Evan Bonds. The people can't very well believe this cock-and-bull story made up of circumstantial evidence. Mr. Jellico, where is Evan Bonds?"

Faye Spencer walked over to the defense table and whispered something into Jellico's ear.

"Jellico?"

"A moment, Your Honor."

Under his breath Jellico whispered, "Thank you, Miss Spencer. Thank you for coming back. Now, find Bill and get that sequence of numbers. Harriet has him practicing ball at the high school."

"Your Honor. May I approach?"

"Yes. Let's get on with this. Counselors."

"Your Honor. Mr. Bonds, has been captured in the Ghent Bank Building."

"Mr. Irving, have the police bring him in. I will allow him to be questioned."

"Your Honor, he can't come to us, we have to go to him."

"What? Jellico, you've always liked making a production. Very well, I'll let you. You've never disappointed me yet."

Both attorneys walked back to their tables. In a booming voice Judge Murphy McAdams said, "This court will take a short recess and reconvene at the Ghent Bank Building in thirty minutes."

There were lots of whispers. Questions asked for which no answers were available. More whispering. A few guffaws, some snorts, and a few laughs as everyone headed the three blocks to the Ghent Bank Building.

The judge, both attorneys, Sheriff Shodtoe in handcuffs, bailiff, court reporter, newspaper reporters for the *Marsden County Meteor* and the *Arkansas Gazette*, twelve members of the jury, six alternates, deputy sheriff, and countless interested people gathered in front of the Ghent Bank Building waiting for Bill Potter to bring the key to the front door.

When he arrived, he said, "I only have a key for the back door. We'll have to walk around."

The judge led the way. Everyone else followed in groups of three to five, with the deputy sheriff bringing the defendant. Bill opened the door and stood aside as the throng marched inside. Faye found the light switch and led Jellico, with the horde of onlookers scrambling for a position up close, to the safe. The lights were dim, so Emmett, the only smoker present, lit his cigarette lighter as Bill tried to read a small paper attached to a legal document.

Bill spun the dial on the door to the giant safe, first one way and then another. When he arrived at the last number he turned a large forked brass handle until he heard a loud click and stepped back. Bill retreated farther as more and more spectators pressed forward. He had made it to the back door when he heard the first scream. He heard several more screams and was already outside when people started staggering out holding their noses. Tears came sliding down wet cheeks, some people coughed, others choked on the suffocating stench seeping out after long confinement in the safe.

Jellico was one of the last out, holding onto Faye's arm.

Judge McAdams yelled to the court reporter, "This court is adjourned. We will re-convene Tuesday after Labor Day." To Rafe, or maybe Ralph Johnson he said, "Call the coroner." McAdams stumbled into the alleyway. Looking back, he saw Jellico, "Damn you Jellico."

CHAPTER 24 – STRATEGY

Harriet gave the operator a remembered number, it was time to see if her father had been successful. He was locating a scouting report on the Hotshots from his baseball connections. "Dad, tell me what you've found about the Hotshots. We play Monday."

"Okay, Pumpkin. I was planning on calling you tonight. They're damn good, with few flaws. They've won almost every game they've played, only tying the one against the Israelite House of David. But they win them all the same way: build an early lead, sit on it, and extend it in the ninth. Their pitcher keeps the other team from scoring much and they end up winning by the runs they score in the ninth."

"So they could score more but choose to keep it close in the middle innings. Keep the fans in it, I guess."

"Yeah, that's how I see it."

"So, how about their pitcher?"

"Throws ninety percent curves. Real accurate with the fastball but not much velocity. Doesn't walk many. Averages twelve to fifteen strikeouts per game. Has two curve balls. The first breaks a foot. Biggest curve in baseball, but it stays pretty close to its plane—only dipping three or four inches. The second breaks four to six inches wide and eight inches down, all at the last possible second. Its impossible to hit, but the boy's not all that accurate with it and doesn't pitch it but ten to twelve times a game."

"Dad, we'll not be able to hit him. We been practicing hitting the curve, but our batting practice pitcher only throws a ball that breaks six to eight inches."

"What would help you the most?"

"If I knew when he's going to throw the fastball."

"Okay, when he's going to throw the fastball, he shakes his glove as a signal to the catcher. If he doesn't shake the glove, look for the sweeping curve. If he gets up in the count and thinks he can waste a pitch, he'll throw the sinking curve. Be ready to run on that pitch, because not only is it impossible to hit, it's also impossible to catch.

This James Paul just tries to knock it down in front of him. You should be able to steal a base any time he throws that pitch."

"How about their defense?"

"Rock solid. They have a terrific double-play combination at second and short. If they have any soft spots, it might be weak arms in the outfield. You should be able to advance on any ball hit deep. Oh, and their third base has a strong arm but is a little slow fielding bunts. You might be able to get a few runners by bunting to third."

"Dad, you did a great job. I've now got something to work on. Is there anything else?"

"Well, maybe. This James Paul could probably play pro. Don't give him anything to hit. And Jorge, their centerfielder, is as fast with his legs as any you'll ever see. He bats left and likes to drag bunt. I'd pitch him outside and up a little." A pause. "I think that about does it."

"Thanks, Dad. You've been a big help."

"Hold on, honey. You got to tell me why you decided to do this. You and Bill getting back together?"

"I get whatever I want if I pull the upset."

"Okay, pumpkin, I hope you want what you get."

CHAPTER 25 – THE HOTSHOTS ARRIVE

After playing a game in Blytheville on Friday, the New York Hotshots loaded into their bus and headed for Dancing Deer. The Blytheville Blackhawks had put up a fierce battle but succumbed to a six-run Hotshot rally in the top of the ninth. Before that fateful inning, the lead changed hands three times with the local boys ahead twice. But it wasn't to be, as the six runs propelled the Hotshots ahead by five and out of reach of a tired group of Arkansans.

Since it was Friday, Julius walked down the aisle handing out pay envelopes. When he finished, he walked toward the front where James Paul was driving.

"Here's your pay. Try and keep this thing on the highway. They got awful narrow roads in Arkansas. Guess no one here's ever heard of a shoulder." Julius sat in the seat directly behind James Paul. "Boy. You still sending your ma half your wages?"

"Yes, sir."

"She putting it in savings for you?"

"No. She's gotten sick and can't work. A neighbor takes care of her. I think they use the money I send for food and to keep the fans blowing. It's been a hot summer."

"I know that be right," piped in Jorge Upshaw. He'd joined their troupe in a town just outside Chicago after getting three hits off Spider. Julius thought anybody that could hit Spider on a regular basis needed to be a regular on his team. Julius made an offer.

When James Paul reached the first of the Boston Mountains, he asked if Julius knew anything about their next opponent.

"I've talked with their mayor a couple of times. Their team is brand new. They've only played one game. It's the damnedest thing. I think he wants us to win. He wasn't all that interested in the two-thousand wager, only in what the town would have to fork over. They're going to give us all the gate and all the concession sales. I thought they were going to have some sort of town-wide celebration and were bringing us in for entertainment, but he asked me more than once if I was sure we could beat their Dancing Deer Peckerwoods."

"Ha, ha. Is that what they call themselves?"

"That's the funniest name we've run into yet. Peckerwoods. Ha, ha."

"He says they got a decent pitcher. Throws the ball hard. But not a one of their players can hit. They just try to string together some small ball and hope their pitcher can keep it close. They won their only game with a base hit from some old geezer who knocked the snot out of the ball then couldn't run to first. Ended up falling down and rolling the ninety feet.

"After this game, we're going to take a couple of days off and head to California. Get some rays and dangle our feet in the Pacific."

"Hey. Sounds good to me."

"Me, too."

"This win will make seventy-five. It's time I give you boys a break. We been doing so good, I plan on paying you even though we're not going to be playing. I got some games scheduled starting on the fifteenth, but that's a ways off. Let's spend the weekend drumming up a sizable crowd, whip their butts, and slide out of town with their cash."

The bus got into town an hour before dark. Julius made James Paul drive past the Ritz. He thought the rooms would be too expensive, but had to ask him to come back when he couldn't find other suitable lodging.

Julius said, "Boys, this fancy place is the only one in town. If they charge an arm and a leg we'll have to double up by putting four to a room. I don't want to give them all our earnings for a damn bed."

"We'll manage."

"Well, I ain't sleeping with no Rube Wadell."

James Paul pulled under an awning next to the front door. A uniformed man came over and asked if he could help with their luggage.

"Uh . . . no. We can handle it. You might leave the cart though."

Julius paid for three nights. He needed three rooms for his players, one for himself and Baby-Doll, and one for her three helpers. He mentally calculated his costs and let out a low whistle. Shaking his head, he stored his bag in his room and headed to the restaurant.

Baby-Doll and her girls were just arriving. He gave the girls a room key and helped get their luggage to a cart. "This is a nice place ladies but don't get too comfortable. We'll be here the weekend, checking out Monday morning before the game. Then, on to California."

Julius deposited Baby-Doll's luggage in his room, then took her downstairs to the restaurant. Lots of people gawked as they strolled by. When they reached the restaurant, a nice-looking man in a suit said there was a thirty-minute wait for a table. He suggested they go into the adjacent cocktail lounge. He'd send a hostess when they could be seated. Actually, the lounge was only separated from the restaurant by a waist-high railing. On the back wall stood a massive oak bar extending down the wall and curving around a corner and out of sight. Julius and Baby-Doll sat in two tall chairs with their feet firmly planted on a large brass cylinder extending from the bar and running down its length twelve inches above the floor. They looked around. The place was filled with chandeliers, gilded mirrors, and a large number of workers wearing crisp clean uniforms.

"Not what you'd expect from a hick town deep in the sticks."

"Julius, have you noticed how many men are wearing jackets? And the women—Julius, the women are wearing evening dresses."

"Yeah, someone needs to tell them that out here they're supposed to wear overalls, with their women in dresses made from flour-sacks."

"Oh, shut up. You could spend some of that money you're stashing away on me. I'd like to have an evening dress."

"Hey, bud. Two beers for me and my lady."

"Julius, I think I want a glass of wine."

"Oh, now, Baby-Doll, you're not going to get uppity on me are you?"

When they finally got seated and were given menus, Julius took a quick look and slowly slid his menu closed and back on the table. "Baby-Doll, this place ain't for us. Let's go find a real place to eat."

"Julius, I want to eat here. A woman can take just so many hamburgers. Open that menu right now and find yourself something to order."

"Okay. Don't throw a hissy-fit." Julius opened his menu and after a moment of silence asked, "Have you ever eaten a French Dip?"

Half-way through the meal a string quartet came onto the stage, the lights dimmed, and an announcer came in from behind a curtain. A spotlight zeroed in as he thumped the microphone. He thanked everyone for coming and announced the quartet. There was polite applause and then the musicians started tuning their instruments. Someone walked up and handed the man a note. He thumped the microphone again and said, "Ladies and gentlemen, the New York Hotshots have arrived."

Julius beamed with pride, as there was substantially more applause for him and his players than there had been for the musicians. The spotlight panned the room and settled on a large group of men sitting closer to the dance floor than he and Baby-Doll sat. Nine of his ball players were at two tables pushed together. Then the spotlight continued searching and found the remaining three standing up against the bar. Several people were now around his players asking for autographs.

Over the loudspeaker, the announcer said, "Let's see if we have any of the Peckerwoods here."

There were a few snickers and light laughter as the spotlight slowly searched the room, stopping to illuminate first one table and then another. At each place it stopped, the man with the microphone announced a name and deafening applause shook the floor. Most of the men were with their families, with a few sitting together.

"Julius, sit down."

"Damnit, Baby-Doll, they need to know I'm here. Hell, I'm the most important one here.

"Sit down, Julius . . . or I'll sit you down."

"Okay. Okay."

Saturday morning Julius was up, showered, and ready to roll by ten. That was his usual time to get up on days they weren't playing. The room was empty. He quickly toweled dry, put on his last pair of clean clothes and bounded out the door to find Baby-Doll.

Downstairs he saw Baby-Doll's helpers, with one talking to the concierge. "Don't forget, you girls got to get the laundry done today. Here's my key. I'll get another at the front desk."

"We're taking care of the laundry right now."

"And the equipment cleaned and repaired."

"The boys already did that too."

"Where the hell's Baby-Doll?"

The girl handed Julius a colorful brochure listing the amenities the town offered. He opened it up. In the center was an artist's rendering of a map of the city with historical buildings drawn in, as well as streets and other points of interest.

"What's this?"

"She said she'd be where that 'X' is on the map. You could come find her if you were so inclined."

"Oh, all right. But I got to get me a cup of coffee first." He turned and walked toward the restaurant muttering, "Damn woman."

The girl came running. "She also told me to make sure you brought this." The girl handed Julius a brown paper sack.

Outside, he opened the sack. It contained his swimming trunks and hotel towels. Stuffing the sack under his arm and holding a throw-away cup of coffee in one hand, he used his other to open the map. Julius oriented himself with the map. It looked like he needed to turn right and walk ten blocks to some sort of park.

The sidewalk was a wide affair with trees planted on both sides and sometimes in the middle. He passed bright yellow trash cans and one building that looked like a public restroom. He threw away his empty coffee cup in one of the yellow cans and sauntered into the relief station. Inside, the facility was divided into two areas by a tiled wall to the ceiling. On one side were six stalls and a long urinal with flowing water. Mirrors hung above a half-dozen sinks on the tiled wall. On the other side of the same wall were another six sinks with mirrors, and beyond them stood lockers behind teak benches and shower stalls. Julius looked around for a place to put his money or an attendant with a cash box. They should be charging for this.

Back on the street he passed other walkers and looked in several retail store windows. One had a sign announcing a bachelor sale and dance that evening on the courthouse grounds. By the time he saw the park, Julius was in a good mood. This is one pretty little town, he thought.

At the park Julius found a winding pathway criss-crossing a flowing stream. There were several bridges. He stopped at one to look down into the water at white fish wearing patches of brown, red, black, and yellow. Large goldfish with long gossamer fins slowly undulated and propelled bulging eyes and bright golden torsos around the rocks and potted plants. Fragrant flowers grew right out of the water and filled the air with a sweet intoxicating smell. Tables had inlaid checkerboards. Benches were conveniently located near pools of water. And mists of water cooled the air and jetted at any walkers lucky enough to be caught in their midst. In the background Julius could hear the distant rumble of large diesel motors.

While looking into the water from the midway point of an arching bridge, Julius felt an arm reach through his. "I think this is the prettiest little town we've been to. Did you bring our swim suits?"

Julius held up the sack. "Yours in here too?"

"Yeah, I had no idea when I left the hotel this morning. I had to call and get one of the girls to gather them up for us. Here, let me show you what I've found."

Julius and Baby-Doll held hands as they walked the remaining hundred feet to the pool. They went into a dressing room and changed into swimming outfits. An elderly attendant took their street clothes and gave them keys to a locker for a dime each. When they emerged from the dressing area they walked down a twisting pathway to a pool. In the back several people stood under a waterfall. A narrow rock wall barely jutted above the water partitioning the pool of water into two sections. They stepped into the first area, where the water was still and quiet. It was also hot. After letting out a gasp, Julius reached behind the rock wall divider and felt cool water. He thought about jumping over the partition, but by this time, his body had started to adjust, and he just wanted to find a rock to sit on and let the hot water purge his body of its aches and pains.

"What do you think, Julius?"

"I think I'm in Cuba."

"Oh, really? And where in Cuba would you find something like this?"

"I don't know. Havana, maybe. But I could close my eyes here and be in any place I wanted."

A few minutes later, Julius saw a woman go to a jug suspended high in the air. She pulled a chain and a stream of water poured in a graceful arc. The pretty, young woman opened her mouth and drank. Julius slid from his rock and headed for the water. When he pulled the chain, the water he tried to drink was hot. Even hotter than the water he was standing in. When he came back, Baby-Doll was sitting on his rock.

"Man, that water was good. It might have a little peppermint added to it somehow. Baby-Doll, we got to get some jugs of that to take with us when we go."

"Why didn't you bring me back a cup?"

"I didn't see any cups."

Baby-Doll slid off the rock and walked across the sandy bottom to the hot water jug. Julius assumed his original position on the rock, thinking women can be led so easily.

Julius and Baby-Doll stayed in the hot water as long as they could, then slipped across a stone staircase over the partition and into the cooler water on the other side. Somehow during their stint in the hot water, an arctic blast had turned the cooler water into something icebergs could have lounged in comfortably. Baby-Doll challenged Julius to stand under a second waterfall. Julius shivered. His body shook so violently, he wasn't aware his swimming trunks had slid to his ankles. Baby-Doll laughed and pinched his butt.

She whispered, "If you don't pull up your swimming trunks I'll be the envy of every woman in town."

Julius scrambled to get his trunks pulled up and then sat on a rock, more than a little embarrassed.

"Julius, we got to get you out of this town. Your inhibitions are slinking off, leaving behind a nice man no one would recognize."

Back in the dressing room, the attendant said, "Are y'all with the ball players from New York?"

Julius beamed. "Yes. I own the team."

"I hope you enjoy your time here. I was passing through a few years back and decided this was as close to paradise as I was like to find. Actually, it was my wife who said she wasn't budging and for me to start looking for a job.

"I hear your boys ain't lost a game. How you gonna handle defeat?"

"The Peckerwoods good enough to beat us?"

"Ha, ha. Peckerwoods. You got a sense of humor too, but I'd be careful about using that name." The attendant reached for their keys. "To answer your question. No, they're not good enough to beat the Hotshots. 'Course, you got to play our team, but it's Bill Potter you got to look out for. Ain't nobody beats him at anything."

"And this Bill Potter. Does he own the team?"

"Oh no, sir. The team represents the town. If anyone owns them, she does. But Bill Potter's on the team and he more or less calls the shots. I've heard stories about him you would not believe."

"What kind of stories?"

"You know, I got to get back to work, but I'll surely be at the game. The entire town's going to be there. I hear several busses are coming in from Skunk Hollow as well. So you'll have your supporters."

"From Skunk Hollow?"

"Yep. They're the ones we beat on Independence Day. They didn't take it so well either."

"Well, here's enough to buy you and your missus a hot dog at the game."

Julius handed the man a dollar and he and Baby-Doll left the dressing room to take a further tour of the town. Outside, Julius heard the low rumble of diesel engines again. He asked a pedestrian what was being built.

"Our new baseball ballpark."

"The Peckerwoods going to have their own stadium?"

"Peckerwoods? Where'd you hear that name?"

Julius shrugged.

"Well, sir, that's a local term of endearment. Being an outsider—you're with the Hotshots, right?—being an outsider you would do well to refer to them as the Men from Dancing Deer."

Farther along the street they stopped to peer into the window of Creighton's Jewelers. As if in a trance, Baby-Doll slowly let go of Julius' hand and walked inside.

Julius called out, "Now, Baby-Doll. Don't go in there." But, it was to no avail. When Julius entered the store, he saw she was looking in the jewelry case holding wedding rings.

After their noon meal, Baby-Doll and her girls had scheduled manicures, pedicures, and facials at Gena's Salon on the first floor of the Ritz Hotel. Julius got a local paper and headed outside to find a park bench under a shade tree.

He read an article about his Hotshots and saw pictures of his boys playing the Blytheville Blackhawks just two days before. There were stills of each player, their names, fielding positions, and statistics. He wondered how the paper got the pictures. He hadn't seen any cameras. If someone kept up with his team, they could figure the stats, but then again who would have the patience . . . and the know-how.

In the center of the paper were pictures of the Men from Dancing Deer. It looked like they went to a photography studio to have their pictures taken. Beside each picture was a name and personal information but nothing to let the reader know he was a ballplayer except his expected fielding position The next page was a score card with a picture of a playing field. Stick men were drawn and position numbers given. At the bottom of the page were instructions for scoring the game. Julius got up and headed back into the hotel. He needed more papers. Along the way he asked the concierge where the Men from Dancing Deer practiced.

"I don't know, sir."

"Well, where will the ball game be played?"

"Ridley Field won't be completed for a while, so I guess it'll be at the high school field, like their game with the Polecats."

"And where is that?"

The man at the desk pulled out another brochure and pointed to a spot on the city map.

"Thanks. Here, buy yourself a couple of hot dogs at the game." Julius handed the man a dollar.

He then bought every paper stacked beside the restaurant's cash register. After depositing them in his room, Julius headed to the high school.

Julius saw the school perched on the top of a hill and walked up a winding path to its summit. To one side of the school was a plain-vanilla ball field. From a rock outcropping you could see the town in the distance. With his back facing town Julius carefully documented the battlefield in his mind. A backstop curved twenty feet behind home plate and stood in front of five small stands of bleachers. It looked like a new chain-link fence had been erected to keep the fans off the field. The new fences went down the first and third base paths and skewed out, giving more room in foul territory as they progressed. Just before the fences reached even with first and third sat two benches. This would be where the ball players would sit. In the distance, down the left field fence, stood a score board where young men would place placards on pegs for runs scored. Several men pushed lawnmowers in the outfield.

To another observer Julius asked, "Have they practiced today?"

"Nope."

"Are they any good?" Julius thought he knew the answer but would have felt better had he been able to have seen them practice.

"Yep."

"Do you think they'll be able to beat the New York team?"

"Yep."

"You, sir, are a man of many words."

"Yep."

On the way back to the hotel Julius saw more signs posted to light-posts and bulletin boards. The town was getting ready for a street dance and everyone was invited. This particular street dance was an annual event always held the Saturday before Labor Day.

The town blocked off Main Street and auctioned off its bachelors. Women secretly nominated the ones they wanted to vote on, and all afternoon vigilante committees of the town's women went around gathering up the nominees. Games and entertainment on the courthouse grounds were provided so the bachelors wouldn't feel put out while they waited for the festivities to begin.

There was a knocking on the door. Spider put down his cards. "Nobody look. I'll see who's at the door and bring back sodas.

"Can I help you ladies?"

"A Mr. James Paul has been nominated. We've come to collect him."

"I beg your pardon."

"Is there a man named James Paul here?"

"Uh . . . no. He's in the next room over." Spider jerked his thumb to his left.

"Thank you, sir. You gentlemen are all invited. There's no cover charge. Just bring your dancing shoes. Refreshments and complimentary food will be provided but no alcohol. We have strict rules about where we allow the drinking of alcohol. Come on down. The festivities starts at seven, but games are already laid out and there are some food items for the bachelors we've previously deposited. Join us, you'll have a good time."

"Hurry, girls. Clarice's team already has one. We got to get this one and find where the Peckerwoods are stashed."

The women knocked on the next door and in a few minutes had James Paul in their clutches. They were walking him down the hall when another young lady ran up saying the Peckerwoods were hiding in the stairwell. The ladies ran for the stairs, dragging James Paul and followed by eleven Hotshot players wondering what was going on.

One team of ladies charged up from the bottom floor as the team bringing James Paul descended from the third. The helpless ball players caught in the middle wondered, if they broke out a window and jumped, would it be worth it? While they pondered this, both groups of ladies converged. It was mayhem, as first one and then another bachelor was caught. Wally, Bear, and Leonard were separated from the married men and carted off.

By six o'clock most of the Dancing Deer bachelors sat in front of the Marsden County Court House playing checkers, eating *hors d'oeuvres*, and drinking iced tea. In another hour they would be auctioned off to the widows, the spinsters, the lonely, the lovely—the women of Dancing Deer. The city police was there to see nothing awkward happened and that the men fulfilled their obligations. The money made was destined for Saint Bartholomew's Orphanage.

"James Paul, what you doing, boy?"

"I don't know, Mr. Mosivido. They said I've been nominated. One man said I'd probably be snapped up by some old spinster and have to dance with her all night."

"I don't think you'll be the worse for wear. But don't eat anything that'll make you sick. Make sure you only eat and drink from the same containers as everyone else. I'd hate to think this was a trick to get my star catcher too sick to play Monday."

"Good Lord, Julius. Let the boy have some fun. Would it be so bad if someone actually beat your vaunted boys? I mean, you gotta lose sometime. Get that monkey off your back."

"I don't want to lose here—or anywhere."

"You gotta lose once before you play those Monarchs. Otherwise everyone will be so uptight they won't be able to play their best game. And you know it'll take their best game to beat the best of the colored league."

"Yeah, well, you let me worry about that." Julius turned to James Paul. "Boy, have a good time but don't get hurt."

Emmett Irving was brought forward and deposited with the younger men. A woman came up complaining that Wally Braxton, brought in with the other Peckerwoods, was her man.

"But you're not married. So that makes him eligible and someone has shown an interest. Maybe this other person won't step forward and you can buy him for the dollar minimum."

"I should've married him when he asked."

At six, a hillbilly band started setting up. A woman walked to a microphone and said she was the master of ceremonies. She announced the rules: a meal at eight, and three hours of companionship from nine until midnight. No man would be required to do anything other than to eat, talk, and to dance occasionally with his purchaser. All money would be donated to charity and if anyone gave any problem, whatsoever, they would spend the night in the hoosegow—man or woman—separated, of course. Several people laughed. One man had to be slapped on his back. He'd been drinking when the woman talked of a jail sentence and his beverage went down the wrong pipe.

The first man auctioned was Leonard from the ball team. Two young ladies, about his own age, got into a spirited battle. When the

146

amount reached forty dollars, one young lady's father nodded his approval and she jumped the bid to sixty. The other young lady sat down.

The master of ceremonies stuck her hand into a jar and pulled out James Paul's name. The young lady losing the bid for Leonard was the first to voice an opening bid for James Paul. She ended up winning and saved fifteen dollars.

When Daniel Poul's name was drawn, Gena offered twenty dollars. One of Baby-Doll's helpers countered with twenty-five, and the race was on. When the dust settled the girl from the Hotshots gathered up money from her two friends and ten more from Baby-Doll. Mr. Poul had been purchased by a pool of Hotshots. He was in for a wild evening.

Emmett Irving was purchased by old man Ridley's grand-daughter and so it went as one bachelor after another was auctioned and led offstage by his purchaser. When Bear's name came up he was asked to take off his shirt. Now, Bear was the biggest man in Dancing Deer at six foot seven. He also weighed three hundred pounds, but on such a large frame it didn't appear to be fat. When he removed his shirt there was a collective gasp as he showed a taut stomach, broad shoulders, and massive arms. He looked like a body builder with hair. A prospective purchaser asked if he had a swim suit handy, but the master of ceremonies didn't hear as she asked a man to find something heavy. She started the bidding at forty dollars. The second bid was for a hundred and Katy wondered if they'd take a check. She bid a hundred and twenty dollars and was quickly raised by thirty to a hundred and fifty by Baby-Doll.

"Baby-Doll, what the hell are you doing? You're with me, honey."

"Oh, I'm sorry, Julius. I got carried away. Did you say the magic word?"

"Uh . . . no. Baby-Doll, what would that word be?"

"Sorry, Julius." She turned to the master of ceremonies, raised her hand, and said, "Two hundred."

The woman on stage turned to Bear. "Mr. Radisson, would you be so kind as to turn your back to the audience. Everyone wants to see how tiny your . . . uh, waist might be. Okay, now walk from one end of the stage to the other and back again." She held out his shirt. "Here, sling this." She then looked at the band. "Can we have some traveling music?"

The women went crazy. A man walked up carrying an anvil. "Is this okay? I had it in the back of my truck."

"I've got two hundred. Do I hear two-fifty? Yes two-fifty over on the left."

Katy looked to her right. Who's bidding? Must be the woman with the short brown bob. The woman on stage looked at Katy and said, "Two seventy-five?"

Katy nodded. She reached into her purse for her checkbook. Two hundred and seventy-five dollars was a lot of money for something she might could wrangle for free, but part of her reasoning was to stifle the competition.

The lady on stage said, "I'm bid two seventy-five. Do I have three hundred? Yes, I've now got three hundred. She turned to Bear, "Mr. Radisson, will you kindly lift up this little anvil? These women want see if you're as strong as you look."

The man struggled to the center of the stage carrying the heavy object. He had to slowly lower it so as not to let it slip. After depositing the heavy object at Bear's feet he wiped the sweat from his brow and backed off. Bear reached down, grabbed the anvil by its horn, and picked it up with his right hand. The muscles in his forearm stood out and glistened with a small amount of perspiration. He twisted it so the weight was directly above his grasp. He then raised it over his head, brought it down to his waist, changed hands, twisted it again, turning it down, and lowered it to the floor with his left. There was an angry thud when the anvil hit the floor.

"Four hundred dollars."

"I'll go four-fifty."

Katy braced herself. She raised her hand, "Five."

"I'm bid five hundred. Do I hear six? Six? No? Five fifty . . . five fifty? Five twenty-five? No? Going once . . . twice . . . sold for five hundred smackers."

Katy went to the stage, wrote out a check to the orphanage, and walked off leading her purchase.

"Kate, wait a minute. I've got to get my shirt."

Buttoning the last button and sliding it into his pants Bear said, "I don't know how to dance. Can we just talk?"

After the last bachelor was sold the band started thumbing banjos and strumming guitars while everyone present sat to eat a meal of fried chicken. One man blew into a jug while another played a harmonica. A young girl sang accompanied by a fiddle. It would be a night everyone would remember for a long time.

The next day was Sunday. Julius, his players, Baby-Doll, and the girls were eating breakfast when it started. At first one person and sometimes two walked down the sidewalk. Both the men and women wore hats. Quite a number had bibles tucked under their arms. They walked down the street with a purpose—a place to be. At a few minutes after ten the sidewalks filled, carrying most of the town to assorted churches. Julius and his boys talked and paid little heed, but Baby-Doll and her girls were glued to the windows like appliqués.

They were told the town pretty much closed on Sunday. No retail stores were open. The restaurants were open, but hardly anything else. Julius and his boys played dominoes in one of the rooms. James Paul oiled his glove and thought about his date the previous night. He had a telephone number and an address. He might come back in the winter. The girls giggled. They had a nice time with Daniel. They were of the opinion he had as well. Several times he tried to dance with all three at the same time. So the girls thought back, giggled, and worked. They prepared their treats to be sold in the concession stands. They had coolers of wrapped dry ice to keep their work refrigerated. Baby-Doll had made arrangements for ice, beverages, condiments, and loaves of bread to be delivered to the ball field in the morning. They knew everything they would buy and everything they could make would be sold. They carried only utensils, spices, and peppers from town to town. From local merchants, they purchased the remaining needed items.

"Does anyone know if they're any good?"

"They can't be. They've only played one game. I mean, we were good individually but didn't play our best ball until we reached Indianapolis. It took us that many games before we played as a coordinated team."

"I know. Still, everyone I've talked to has this sense that somehow they'll pull the upset."

"It won't happen. No one beats us."

"We still planning on playing the Kansas City Monarchs in October?"

"Yeah. It's our last game."

"I think that game will be our big test. We'll find out then if we're as good as we think we are. Satchel Page will pitch. He preaches humility everywhere he goes."

"Satchel is humble?"

"Satchel is a nice guy, but it's his opponents who learn humility."

"Well, let's not be too complacent with these Peckerwoods. They could get lucky."

Julius sat on the edge of the bed listening to his boys. Finally he said, "Here's what we do. We score three runs in the first inning. After that, every time they score one we score two. And then in the top of the ninth, we score five or six. They won't be able to rally enough to overcome those numbers, and if they aren't able to hit Spider, we won't have to score so many runs giving a lopsided score that will embarrass 'em."

There was a knock on the door.

Julius decided it was time to let his team get their rest. He said, "I'll get the door. You guys get some sleep." Julius opened the door. "Yes?"

"You Mr. Mosivido?"

"Yes."

"Mr. Mosivido, I'm the mayor of Dancing Deer. Is there some place we can talk?"

CHAPTER 26 – W.W. WAINWRIGHT

"Love even teaches asses to dance." It was an old French saying and W.W. thought he was willing to give up anything, to do anything—just like the old proverb—if he could be with the woman he loved. But he really wanted her to give up her independence and live with him in New York City.

He tried to reason with her, but she failed to see the enormity of his offer—chief of police for New York City. The pinnacle of his profession. No higher attainment possible. More annual salary than Dancing Deer's entire city budget. What an enormous amount of money. The mayor would only stay in office for one more term—four years. He would retire with all the prestige, the notoriety, the fame, and the money he and Faye could stand. They would then travel the world, stay at fancy resorts, have whatever they wanted. Why couldn't she see that. They had now been apart long enough for her to come to her senses. It was time to go to Dancing Deer, sling her over his shoulder, and bring her back. And if she wouldn't come back, he was prepared to forsake everything offered and stay with her.

W.W. Wainwright settled back in his Pullman car and tried to get some sleep. He felt sure he'd be able to show her the advantages; ask her to give him four years; to live the good life in the Big Apple; and then retire, with a passel of money, to Arkansas. She ought to go for that.

He'd make the most of those four years. He thought about the changes he'd make in the department, the relationship he'd cultivate with the district attorney's office, and the social functions he and Faye would attend. He closed his eyes and saw himself stepping out with a tall, redhead on his arm. Not just any tall redhead, but the vivacious, the devastatingly beautiful, Faye Spencer.

Then he thought about that first night at his sister's, how he turned off the light, undressed down to his drawers, and crawled under a starched sheet. To his left, over the empty expanse of half the bed, he watched as she undressed. She was slow—slow enough for his eyes to adjust. The fan in the window gave off its gentle purr. He saw her remove her dress, her slip, and her bra. He was breathless. She deftly reached around her back with one hand and unfastened it. He thought, I'll have to stay on my side until she's asleep, then I'll crawl over and snuggle against her till morning. She'll wake in my arms. Back on the train, Wayne Winchell Wainwright fell asleep with a smile on his face.

Sometime during the night, a sleepy Appalachian station manager missed pulling a lever that would send a train, loaded down with coal from the West Virginia mines going north, to a side rail so that a Super Chief heading south could pass. The two trains were now on a collision course. Somewhere in West Virginia in mountainous terrain they collided. The Super Chief was almost across a tall trestle spanning a gorge. At the bottom of the gorge flowed a turbulent river. The northbound train had been ascending a long hill and its speed had slowed to a fraction of its normal pace, still, when its conductor saw the southbound train, he could do nothing but blow his whistle and hit the brake. He filled the still dark with shrill peals of terror-stricken noise. Along with the whistle came a generous amount of built-up steam and the screeching of metal brakes pinching the metal rails. The train going north wasn't carrying passengers, only a crew of five and sixty-eight cars of black coal.

The Super Chief's two engines and first five cars buckled on impact and jumped the tracks. The next five cars contained passengers. They also buckled, with three jumping the tracks and two staying atop the trestle at an angle, but not on the tracks. W.W. was thrown from his bed. He got up with a bloody nose and broken glasses. Everything was a haze. Shaking the sleep from his head, he heard women and children screaming and men barking evacuation orders. Those who could, scrambled for an exit. The last two passenger cars perched precariously over the water, the back car teetered. Purses, papers, hats, and luggage fell from the open escape doors.

As people got off, they grouped by family units. One woman screamed her baby girl was still on board. She had to be restrained from returning. W.W. made a motion to the woman with his palm then grabbed a hand rail and pulled himself up and through an open door.

Stumbling through the zigzagged train cars, he passed people unconscious between seats and others who had been trampled in the aisles. A few were trying to make it to the next car forward. W.W. wended all the way back to the last car before he saw a small girl huddled, shaking, beside an elderly man lying on the floor.

"Honey, we have to go. I'll come back and get him after I take you to your mother."

The little girl reached up and put her arms around the chief's neck. He lifted her over the body of the old man. There was a jerk as the wheels on the left side of the car slid off the trestle. The car was now tilted down toward a black hole. W.W. slid out the open escape door clutching the little girl. He could feel his body falling. Vertigo filled his head as he and the little girl hurtled through black nothingness. He held tight to the little girl, cradling her entire body within his. She buried her head in the folds of his nightshirt.

Rescue workers found the little girl clinging to a tree root, her body half in the river and half on a sandy shoal. No one could find the hero who ran back on the train to rescue her.

Papers, luggage, everything was retrieved, sorted, and catalogued. Passenger lists were compared to a list of the survivors. Bodies were identified and those missing were sought. Soon the only passenger not accounted for was W.W. Wainwright, Chief of Police, Dancing Deer, Arkansas.

CHAPTER 27 – THE MEETING

Julius and Mayor Bob went into the bistro. On Sunday only the restaurant portion was open. They went to a table where Julius sat looking over his shoulder at the dark corner separated by the waist-high railing.

"So tell me, Mr. Mosivido, how bad you gonna beat the Peckerwoods?"

"We're going to keep it close until the last inning, then we'll pull away far enough that, with their best efforts, they won't be able to catch us."

"Oh, no. What if they get lucky? You don't know this Bill Potter. He's the sneakiest man you've ever met."

"We aren't going to lose, Mayor. Why do you want us to win so bad if the town gets two thousand dollars if we lose?"

"Uh. Two thousand dollars?"

"Yeah. Two thousand dollars if we get beat in a fair game. But that's not what you want. You got something riding on the game worth more than the two grand, don't you?"

"Uh . . . I feel awful about it, but I bet my tractor and everything I could rake up. The other members of the city council are in the same boat. Bill said if we didn't make the bet he was going to leak the news to the newspaper. He said the voters needed to know the men they elected to manage and promote their town turned against her for thirty shekels."

"But if you declined to place the bet he wouldn't have anything to leak to the newspaper."

"No. You don't understand. Me and the other members of the Dancing Deer City Council bet on the first game, when they played the Polecats from Skunk Hollow. Bill pulled the upset and we lost more than we could afford to lose. Then we tricked him into putting it up double or nothing against the New York Hotshots."

"So if he beats my team, you and the men on the city council—the ones who lost everything they could rake together on the first game—will lose that much more?"

"Uh . . . no. The knave said since we didn't pay the first bet we were all welchers. He said if Dancing Deer lost we were square, but if he somehow won, instead of money he made us sign papers saying we'd do silly things for the town—embarrassing things."

"What kinds of things?"

"My wife, two daughters, and I have to shell and can five hundred pounds of peas. Do you have any idea how many bushels there are in five hundred pounds? Another member and his family have to shuck and can five hundred pounds of corn. Jerry's family has to operate a food pantry all winter long. Bill told the farmers they had to donate food when they came up a little shy on their notes and needed extensions. Also, Stone's a carpenter. He and his family have to build toys to be given out at Christmas time, mostly to the children at Saint Bartholomew's Orphanage. Everyone else, and their families, have to paint every storefront in town."

"Mayor, now you're telling me that if I beat the Men from Dancing Deer, you and your chums are off the hook and the orphans and the poor children of Dancing Deer are not going to have Christmas presents. That this winter, when this pretty little town is covered white with snow, the old, the poor, the displaced are going to starve?"

"You think we should put ourselves out like that? By God, I'm the mayor."

"My team is going to beat the Men from Dancing Deer. And I'm going to give everything I earn from the victory to Mr. Bill Potter to do something nice for this town. Mayor Bob I hope the good people of Dancing Deer run you and your chums out of town in chains. Good evening."

CHAPTER 28 – THE BIG GAME (STARTED)

The day began with the Men from Dancing Deer gathered outside old man Ridley's bedroom. Bill had kept tabs on the old man's progress and thought he might rally if the players dedicated the game to him in person.

"Nurse, we won't be loud. We just want to tell him we're dedicating the game to him and let him know how much he means to us."

"Okay, but he's weak and I won't have you gentlemen causing him any pain. Go on in but keep it down."

"Yes, ma'am."

Ten men in royal blue uniforms with bright yellow trim held their hats and filed into the somber confines of a dying man's bedroom. They took positions around the bed.

"Mr. Ridley . . . Mr. Ridley, are you awake? Mr. Ridley . . ."

The old man's eyes slowly opened. Adelle, his grand-daughter, wiped drool from the corner of his mouth.

Bill spoke for everyone. "Mr. Ridley, sir, today is the day. We play the New York Hotshots in a few hours, but first we want you to know we're dedicating the game to you. No one expects us to win, but no one expected us to beat the Polecats either. And we wouldn't have if you had not provided the winning hit. We're going to give it our best effort. We're playing this one for you, sir."

Mr. Ridley tried to speak but coughed instead. His daughter leaned forward. He started again, but none of the ball players could understand the garbled words. Adelle held his hand and listened intently, occasionally nodding.

"He says, if you can't hit their pitcher, square around to bunt. If the third baseman charges in, punch at the ball like Nelson did in the last game and if he doesn't, lay it down far enough out the pitcher and catcher can't field it. And don't swing at anything not over the plate."

"That's remarkable. His mind is still clear."

157

"Yes. It's his body that's giving out."

"May we call him throughout the game and give him updates?"

"That won't be necessary. Jesse installed a telephone in the announcer's stand. He's planning on giving grandfather the play-by-play. He's rigged up a power supply to our radio and several speakers. The telephone now echoes throughout the room. I'll be listening as well."

The old man pulled on her sleeve. She leaned closer and in a minute she said, "He says if you don't beat them damn New Yorkers, he's going to move his money to that bank in Skunk Hollow."

Bill would later swear he heard old man Ridley laugh. The nurse came in and said, "You gentlemen need to leave now or Mr. Ridley won't have enough strength to listen to the game. And that's what's keeping him alive."

Each man shook Torguson Ridley's hand and filed out. Bill was the last one. "Good-bye, sir."

At ten the Men from Dancing Deer were in the strategy room getting last-minute instructions from Harriet.

"I want to make sure everyone knows the signs and I have a few to add. We've been over these a hundred times, but once more won't hurt and I don't want anyone's mind to go blank when the moment arrives."

It was a solemn group of men, sitting on the edge of their chairs, who nodded agreement. Harriet went through a series of motions, each one different. No one said a thing. She put her hand on her hip and with the other touched her belt buckle.

"Hit and run."

"That's right. The only sign that works is the one given when I've got this hand on my hip. How about this one?"

"Bunt."

"Hit away."

"Take the next pitch."

"Steal."

"And I want to add this one." She put on a pair of sunglasses. "Here it is." She used her free hand to push her glasses further back on her dainty nose. "This means the next pitch is going to be a fastball

158

somewhere over the plate. You need to swing at it. He doesn't have a fastball like Jed. This is more like the one thrown by Daniel. Nothing against your fastball Daniel, but you men should be able to hit this pitch. And this one." She took her sunglasses off and held them in her free hand. "This means you'll not be able to hit the next pitch. You should take it. I'm not going to tell you to absolutely take it, but it'll probably be outside the strike zone. He's not very accurate with this pitch and you need to be thankful for that, 'cause you can't hit it. You might consider swinging if you're down in the count with two strikes. That way you can run to first and try and beat the throw from the catcher, because not only is it unhittable, it's also uncatchable."

"Now let's talk about how they play the game. In the games they've played so far they've scored four or five runs in the first two innings. Then they coast till the ninth only scoring if their opponents score. In the top of the ninth, they score an additional four or five. It's then out of reach for their unlucky adversaries. We need to keep them from scoring that four or five in the first two innings. That'll discombobulate them. It'll affect their play for the remainder of the game. And we want to pace ourselves. Of course we'll play to the best of our abilities at all times, but in the eighth we're going to pull out all the stops. We're going to make them have to score in their top of the ninth to stay with us. Any comment?"

Leonard raised his hand. "I just want to say that I hope to God we beat these Hotshots, but if we don't, I'm still proud to be on the team."

"Here, here."

"Me, too."

"All we can do is play the best we can. No one expects us to win. And it won't be embarrassing if we lose. But I think we're ready and I don't think the Hotshots have played a team more determined, more disciplined, or more supported than the one they're up against today. Let's go, men."

When the Men from Dancing Deer left the strategy room, they walked down the marble hallway trying to stay on the Persian rugs so their metal cleats would be muffled. A few fans waited in the bistro. These fans joined the team and walked with them through the door. Outside the Ritz Grand Hotel and Ballroom more fans waited.

Additional people joined as the throng marched in a somber procession down the sidewalk. Some of the ballplayers walked on the grass. When they reached the wide, winding path leading to the school their metal cleats crunched in the small pebbles. Pride swelled in the town for the Men from Dancing Deer.

The New York Hotshots watched from their windows. Spider said, "Boys, I think we got us a game."

Julius slowly shook his head. He said, "After we win, we better cry with the losers and commiserate with the fans or they'll be escorting us out of town in vats of tar."

At eleven, a U. S. Postal worker handed a first-class letter to Faye from W.W. He said he loved her. He couldn't live without her. He would arrive sometime on Labor Day and they would decide what to do. If she was adamant about staying in Dancing Deer, he would give up the idea of being New York City's chief of police, or if she could tolerate being away from home for four years, he'd agree to move back to Dancing Deer and let her continue her career when the mayor's term was over.

Faye cried as she read the letter. Of course she'd go back with him. They might retire to Dancing Deer, but there was nothing wrong with living life in the fast lane for a while. Being chief of police would mean so much to W.W. It was selfish of her not to have seen that. And then there was her new career as an author. New York City was where she could do it the most good. What had she been thinking? Now she berated herself for not being the first one to mend the fences. W.W. Wainwright was the man. She'd waited for him her whole life. She'd be there when he got off the bus.

Faye went straight to the bus station to find out what times the busses arrived. On Sundays and holidays they operated on a reduced schedule. She was told the first bus of the day arrived from Little Rock at three in the afternoon. Another arrived at eleven that night. No other busses until Tuesday when they would be back to their regular schedule of one every six hours from Little Rock and two daily from Russellville.

The Men from Dancing Deer stood in front of their benches down the third base line. The Hotshots took infield practice with Spider and James Paul playing catch between the foul line and their bench.

Julius said, "Let's get one." He tossed the ball in the air and hit a grounder to third. The ball was scooped up and a bullet fired to first. The next went to short. When it was first's turn the ball made him run toward the pitcher's mound to field it. He turned and tossed it to the second-baseman covering his bag.

From the bench behind third base a Peckerwood said, "Whew. They don't ever bobble the ball. You see how their feet are always in the right position to catch it and then it's a quick pivot, one step, and a throw. They are slick."

Next the Hotshots practiced their double-play routines, the play at home, and third and first fielded bunts. After these two scooped their bunt and flipped to second covering first, they headed to the bench.

Julius yelled out, "Left, take it to second." He then hit a fly ball to left field, where the fielder caught the ball and threw to second.

"Now, bring it home." Julius hit another fly to left and this time the fielder caught the ball and threw it to home plate letting the ball bounce one time before being caught.

Julius did the same to center and to right, then said, "All right, come on in." The Hotshots ran to their bench and waited to see how the Men from Dancing Deer stacked up.

Harriet wore a bright yellow sundress, open-toed sandals, a wide-brimmed hat tied under her chin with a matching yellow scarf, and sunglasses. She didn't give infield practice. Bill did that. He could hit the ball but was the lousiest fielder on the team, so if he played it would be because someone got hurt or he was needed as a pinch-hitter or pinch-runner. He gave infield practice. They did an admirable job but were not as polished as the Hotshots.

At one in the afternoon, on Labor Day, in the year 1945, the Peckerwoods were set to do battle with the New York Hotshots.

Harriet, Bill, and Julius met at home plate to exchange line-up cards. Harriet held out her hand. "I'm Harriet Potter. Welcome to Dancing Deer."

"Ma'am, are you the manager?"

"Yes, I am. Do you have a problem with that?"

"No, ma'am."

"Are you Julius Mosivido?"

"Yes, ma'am."

"Let me introduce you to my husband, Bill Potter, and the three umpires. They are the youngest ministers in town and all three have been studying the rules. I believe your communication with the mayor requested them in preference to regular umpires."

"Yes, ma'am."

"Pastor Moore will be behind the plate. And Pastor Williams behind first with Pastor Wright behind third. Do you have any questions?"

"No, ma'am."

Harriet gave a hand signal and Father Donovan O'Reilly from Saint Bartholomew's Holy Catholic Church stepped to the microphone and began to sing "The Star Spangled Banner" a cappella, his voice a rich tenor with an Irish brogue. A slight breeze lifted the flag. It was a good time to be an American, to be in beautiful Arkansas, and especially in the small, proud town of Dancing Deer. The war was closing down. The boys were coming home. It was a splendid day. And the hometown heroes were about to pummel the New York Hotshots. The people of Dancing Deer were ecstatic. Tears welled in their eyes.

When Father O'Reilly finished, the fans wiped their eyes and grabbed their seats as three men and one woman stood at home plate.

Pastor Moore yelled, "Play ball."

After their first week of practice, Harriet moved the players around, saying their skills better matched their new positions. Leonard went to center, Paul Nelson to third, and Big Bear Radisson to first.

Harriet said, "Leonard, you have a strong arm but need time to set your feet before throwing. At the hot box you're not given that time and sometimes your throws have been wide of their mark. Here in center you can use your good fielding ability and fast feet to cover a lot of area and have the time you need to plant your feet before uncorking a strong throw.

"Paul, you're such a good fielder and accurate thrower that third base is your best fit. You're a natural.

162

"And you, Bear, are such a big man, you make quite a target for the other fielders. Also, you don't ever let anything get through. Now that you have a decent first baseman's mitt, you haven't made an error.

"Wally, you and Daniel have new gloves. They're smaller than anyone else's because you have to transfer the ball to your throwing hand faster than anyone else. But it should be easier to catch grounders with the fingers laced together."

And, indeed, Harriet was right—as usual. The men caught on to their new positions and their new gloves. It was one of the first changes Harriet made and it was one of her best.

The lead-off batter for the Hotshots watched as the first ball came slid the center of the plate. David had guessed he wouldn't be swinging, wanting to see what kind of pitch Jed could throw, so David asked for the off-speed fastball. It was Jed's best new pitch and he had no problem splitting the plate with it. Strike one. The batter, thinking Jed's fastball wasn't all that fast, swung too late on Jed's second throw, his four-seamer. The Hotshot batter was now down in the count and would have to swing at anything close. Jed was inside with the first and outside with the second succeeding pitch. Neither was close enough to entice the disciplined hitter. Jed then threw his two-seamer. The batter swung but his bat was two inches above the ball when they passed over the plate.

The second man up was Jorge, the center fielder. He batted from the right side of the plate and dragged a bunt between a lunging Jed Calhoun and Bear Radisson. Jed continued on to first. He got there a step ahead of the speedy center fielder, but Wally held on to the ball. It was a perfect bunt. There was no use risking a bad throw, allowing the runner to advance to second, when there was no chance of getting him out.

David called for a four-seam rising fastball. The fleet-foot at first shot for second. The ball was outside. By the time David caught the ball and had it in his hand to throw to second, the runner was already in his slide. The Hotshots were fast—at least the center fielder was.

The third batter hit a line drive to center. Leonard caught the ball on one hop and threw a bullet to home. Bear came over to cut it off but let it go. When the center fielder came sliding home, David was squatting at the plate. He gripped the ball with his bare hand. The hitter advanced to second on the throw. There were now two outs.

David let one down in the dirt get by him and the runner on second ran to third. He scored on a clean single to left. Jed struck out their fifth batter and everyone headed to their bench behind by one run.

Wally was Dancing Deer's lead-off batter. He looked down to Harriet in the third base coach's box. Nothing. The ball came in at his belt and he bailed, landing on his butt. Ten feet in front of the plate the ball started making a flat arc and when it crossed the plate the umpire yelled, "Stee-rike."

Wally thought back to what Harriet said. He should have known that pitch wouldn't hit him. Whoa, the next one's going to be a fastball. Wally swung. He hit a foul ball over his fellow teammates' heads. He thought, "Damn. Got around too fast. Got to pace myself. No signal. Here it comes right down the center." Wally swung but the ball swept outside five inches past the end of his bat. Dejected, he trotted back to the bench. On the way he passed Daniel Poul. "Better pay attention to coach. She's got it figured out and I was too dumb to use it."

Daniel nodded as he went to the plate. He looked to Harriet. A fastball. Daniel was ready and put his bat out at the last second laying down a bunt toward third. The fielder had been playing back and by the time he reached the ball, it was too late. Daniel was now on base with their first base hit.

Leonard was a good hitter and he batted third. He looked to Harriet. Nothing. The ball came down the center. Leonard held his ground and the bat. When the ball passed the plate it had swept far outside. He looked to Harriet. Still nothing. The next pitch was high. Ball two. She went to her sunglasses. A fastball . . . and the hit and run. Daniel got the signal and when the pitcher kicked to home, he tore off for second. The second baseman ran to cover the bag and Leonard waited at the plate on the fastball. It was a little low, but over the outside corner. Leonard hit a grounder to the second baseman's normal position. The ball skimmed through the grass to the right fielder. Daniel rounded second looking at Harriet. She waved her arms for him to keep on motoring. Getting close to third, she held up her hands telling Daniel it wasn't necessary to slide.

With runners on the corners, it was David Blaine's turn. He looked to Harriet. No signal. He was ready and when the ball came over the plate it met the fat part of the bat and shot out between the left and center fielders. He stopped when he got to third, scoring two runs. It was now Abner's turn. He played right field and although he could hit and field decently, he was just an average runner. He looked to Harriet. Fastball. He looked again. Suicide squeeze. What the hell! The pitcher threw from his normal windup. The ball streaked to the plate waist high on the inside portion. Abner lowered his bat and hit the ball inches from his hands. The ball trickled toward the mound. Abner ran for first, not as fast as when he'd been in school, but he was a lot faster than he had been in this last spring. David slid home as the pitcher picked up the ball, pivoted, and threw high to first. The first baseman had to jump to catch it and Abner came hurtling by while the fielder was still in the air.

Jed walked to the batter's box from the on-deck circle. He had spent most of the two months practicing two new pitches and had forsaken much of the team's batting practice. Still he'd been looking forward to taking his turn with the lumber. He looked to Harriet. No signal. He fouled off two, took two that were outside, then waited on the fastball. It was down in the dirt and now the count was full. The next pitch was wide of the plate and Jed trotted to first.

Bear came up to bat with two men on and just one out. He looked to Harriet. Nothing. The ball came straight at him. He waited, expecting to be hit. It was a big part of his offense. He planned on getting hit. With his frame and all that muscle it would just bounce off and he'd trot to first. But the ball broke flat over the plate.

"Stee-rike."

The pitcher threw the next two pitches outside. The second one was also high. The fourth pitch was right down the middle and Bear had a cut that would have sent the ball past the city limits if he'd connected. But he didn't, as the ball curved six inches outside the plate. That made it two and two. He didn't want to strike out. Where was that fast ball? The next pitch came straight at his knees. This is the one that'll break over the plate. He stayed in the batter's box and swung smooth, going down after it. There was a crack of the bat and a low liner inches above the ground shot out on the right side of the infield. The first baseman caught the ball on one hop, turned, and threw to second. Short covered the bag and threw back to first. A slow Bear Radisson was still ten steps shy of first when the first baseman caught the ball while standing on the bag. He tossed the ball underhanded toward the mound and ran off the field. They needed to score some runs.

In the top of the second, the Hotshots' left fielder hit a homerun with no one on base. They also had one strikeout and two grounders to third. Paul Nelson fielded both balls cleanly and threw strings to Bear Radisson. After two opportunities, the Hotshots were normally ahead by several runs. Against the Men from Dancing Deer, they were behind by one and their opponents were now up for their second effort.

Paul Nelson looked at Harriet. She gave several signals. No hand on the hip, so none counted. The ball came down the middle and he swung. Nothing but air. He fouled off the next one and quickly found himself down in the count. Harriet took off her sunglasses. The pitch no one could hit. Paul watched as the ball came to the outside part of the plate. It curved and dipped at the last second. A little blip. The ball had a hitch in its step. She's right—no one could hit that thing. Paul wondered how she knew what was being tossed, but thanked whatever powers there are that she knew. With one ball and two strikes Paul squared to bunt. The third baseman charged in and Paul punched hard at the ball. It went straight at the third baseman but was too hot for him to handle at fifteen feet from the plate. The ball bounced off his body into the Men from Dancing Deer. Pastor Moore called time and awarded Paul second base.

Amos, Dancing Deer's left fielder, came to bat next. He squared to bunt, but this time the third baseman held back. Amos didn't hit so good so he'd spent a lot of time practicing his bunts. He sent the ball trickling just inches inside the third base line. The Hotshot third baseman had no play other than to let it roll. Maybe it would hit something and go foul. No such luck. Now there were two runners on and still no outs.

Wally walked to the plate. This time he knew what to do. The first pitch came in at his knees. Wally stood his ground, he didn't bail. He swung and lined a double over the third baseman's head.

Paul rounded third and scored easily. A slow Amos made it to third and Wally pulled up at second. He'd made up for that first time to the plate.

Daniel was swinging out of his socks and went back to the bench after three efforts.

Leonard came up with runners on second and third. Julius yelled something from the bench and Spider gave him an intentional walk. They were going for the double play.

David Blaine came up and missed badly at two curve balls. Harriet gave him a signal. The next pitch would not be hittable. Damn. It wasn't and neither was it catchable. The ball bounced off James Paul's leg a short way toward first.

Amos had been told to take a gigantic lead toward home and to go in if the catcher missed the ball. James Paul raced after the ball and charged back to the plate but too late to get the lumbering Amos. Wally advanced to third and Leonard to second.

David Blaine hit a shallow pop-up to left field off the end of his bat. It landed fifteen feet in front of the left fielder, and Wally came home.

Abner hit a line shot to first, who caught the ball and stepped on first doubling off a flat-footed David Blaine.

At the end of two full innings of play the Men from Dancing Deer were ahead of the New York Hotshots six to two. Julius decided he needed to have a talk with his battery. "James Paul, she's stealing your signs. They're swinging at every fastball Spider throws."

"I don't give the signs, Mr. Mosivido. Spider gives me the signs."

Julius looked at Spider. "Okay, she's figured out your sign for fastball. You have to let James Paul start giving the signs. He should've been doing it all along. You gotta concentrate on pitching. Let James Paul keep up with the strategy."

Julius turned to his hitters while Spider and James Paul started going over the new signal arrangement. "What's with you guys, anyway?"

"He's good, Julius. He's got three different fast balls and he's accurate with all three."

"Then, lets start bunting. We got to stop the blood and inch our way back into the game. I agree he's got good stuff, but he's also got a slow delivery and not a very good pick-off move. We need to steal some bases. James Paul is up fourth this inning. Let's give him some base runners."

Mr. Ridley had talked his grand-daughter and the nurse into propping him up in bed. They sat in chairs and the three of them listened to Jesse give his play-by-play.

"The Hotshots are down six to two with their second baseman up first. He struck out his first at bat."

A loud crack pierced the afternoon heat and the radio.

"Amos runs for the left field foul pole. The ball lands in fair territory and heads to places unknown. Amos gives chase. He's got it. A long throw back in. Daniel cuts off the ball and fires home. Safe. The runner slid in under David's tag. The Hotshots have now cut Dancing Deer's lead to three. Their center fielder walks to the plate. He bunted last time up and was thrown out at the plate by a strong throw from Leonard, the center fielder. He bats left. He squares and pulls the ball to first, Bear runs in, bare-hands the ball, and flips to Wally covering the bag. Whew, that guy is fast. He's safe at first by a mile."

There was some shuffling of papers then, "Katy what's the name of their shortstop?"

"Carlos."

"Carlos walks to the plate, takes a few practice swings, and waits on the ball. Jed pitches from the stretch. Comes to set and throws to first. The runner dives back head first. Jed starts his wind, comes to set, looks to first again, kicks, and comes home. Carlos gives a big swing, fouling off the ball into the stands. He steps out, hits his cleats with the bat, steps back into the batter's box, scratches out dirt like a cat covering scat, and stands ready. Jed comes to set, throws the ball to first. He's caught the runner leaning toward second, and they now have him in a run-down. Bear takes a few steps and tosses to Wally, the runner stops and heads back to first, passes Bear who steps out of the way, Wally tosses to Jed who's now covering first. Jed tags him out. Man, what a play. This is just like the bigs."

Old man Ridley clapped his hands, tried to say something, and started coughing. Adelle brought him a glass of water. She held it as he drank. She then wiped what he dribbled down his chin. "You enjoying the game, Grandfather?"

Mr. Ridley nodded his head and motioned for more water.

When James Paul came up to bat, Carlos was on second. He'd walked and stolen the base. James Paul hit a ball that got by Abner in right, and Carlos scored. Jed struck out the next two batters, leaving James Paul stranded on second. The Hotshots were closing and now were two back, with the Men from Dancing Deer coming to bat in the bottom of the third.

Jed was first up. He looked at Harriet. No signal. Must be a curve. The ball came straight at him, he got ready to swing expecting the pitch to start curving over the plate. It didn't break and hit Jed in his arm. A yellow streak came in from third.

"Jed, are you all right? Let me see that arm."Harriet was in the middle of everything. She turned to the umpire. "He needs to be warned. He can't start throwing at our players. That's no way to win a game. Jed's our pitcher. He hit him in his throwing arm, for God's sakes."

The umpire walked to the mound. "Son, I don't think you intentionally meant to hit Jed, but if you hit another batter, and it appears to me you did it on purpose, I'll throw you from the game. Do you understand?"

"Yes sir, I do. But why didn't he move out of the way. He just stood there like he wanted to get hit."

"I see your point, but you throw such a wide-sweeping curve he probably thought it would start breaking and slide over the plate. This will be your only warning."

"Yes, sir."

Jed was now on first and someone gave him a royal blue jacket to keep his arm from cooling off too fast, stiffening up. Bear Radisson came up. He looked to Harriet. Fastball. Hot dog. Bear was ready. The ball came sailing down the middle and just about the time that Bear started his swing, the ball curved out of the strike zone. What the hell? Bear looked at Harriet. She had hands on both hips. What was that a signal for?

Bear got ready again. This time he hit the pitch, slapping the ball toward the third baseman. He threw to second, with the second baseman throwing to first after he raked his foot across the top of the bag. Three innings, two times to bat, and two double plays. Bear was not having a good day at the plate. Paul flied to left, and after three innings the Men from Dancing Deer were ahead six to four.

CHAPTER 29 – FAYE

Faye got up from her seat in the bleachers and headed to the concession stand. She'd get a soda for the hot walk down the hill to town. It was time to meet the arriving bus from Little Rock. W.W. will get to see the last half of the game. She thought he might've been playing if they'd not gone to New York two months earlier. As she walked along she mused over what position he would play. They'd have to go see some games at Yankee Stadium. See Joltin' Joe DiMaggio.

The mayor could make a big deal out of it and engender fan support. They'd probably sit in a box with a great view. Maybe meet some of the players. Get their autographs. A ball maybe.

When the bus arrived she walked outside. Faye watched each passenger get off. No W.W. Wainwright. She went back inside and asked the lady in charge if a W.W. Wainwright would arrive on the eleven o'clock bus.

"Ma'am, there's no way for me to know. We don't make reservations. No one has assigned seating or anything."

"I know, I'm just worried something happened to him. Now that I've made up my mind, I have this sickening feeling I might be too late."

"Made up your mind about what, honey?"

Faye had talked with Katy for only the briefest period of time. Since she was staying with the ball team at the Ritz and keeping a curfew, Faye had not had an opportunity to tell her how she had fallen in love with W.W. What's with her, anyway? Why was she staying with the ball team? They would have time tonight to talk about it, but in the meantime Faye felt an affinity with the bus lady and said, "I've been shying away from serious relationships for years while I got my career going. Now I've decided to balance the two and the man I've chosen was supposed to have been on that bus. I have this sickening feeling I waited too long to find him. You don't think anything happened, do you?"

"No, nothing happened. 'Course, they did have that train that derailed in West Virginia a couple of days ago."

"Derailed?"

"Yeah. A station manager was supposed to pull a switch so a train going north could get on a side rail and let a passenger train pass. Somehow he screwed up and kept it going north. The north-bound train carrying freight had a head-on collision with a south-bound Super Chief. Several passengers and even some of the crew were killed."

"How'd you hear about the accident?"

"I'll get the paper. It was in yesterday's *Gazette*."

Faye waited while the bus lady left her station. She probably had the paper in her car. In a few minutes she was back, folding, unfolding, inserting, and reinserting sections of the paper.

"Everyone's running sales. Here it is. Look at that picture. Two cars perched atop a trestle and the last car tilted at a severe angle. They say several people fell out of the second car into the water."

Faye took the paper. She started reading, then skimmed through, looking for his name. Three quarters through she found it. Wayne Wainwright's body has not been found. Faye slumped in her chair. With tears streaming down her face, she ran from the bus station, her hand clutching the paper.

CHAPTER 30 – THE BIG GAME (FINISHED)

Nothing much happened in the fourth, fifth, and sixth innings. Both teams managed to get a base runner or two, but no runs scored. Bear hit into another double play in the sixth and James Paul gunned down Daniel trying to steal second. Otherwise, it had turned into a pitcher's duel.

After Bear hit into his third double-play, Mr. Ridley got agitated and excitedly wanted Adelle to do something for him.

"Grandfather, you'll have to talk slower so I can understand what you're saying."

"Yes, I know where it is. You want me to take it where? Right now?"

In ten minutes, Adelle walked up the winding pathway to the high school. She heard the crowd in the distance. When she arrived, no one took her entrance fee so she walked through the gate and headed to the walkway behind the fence separating the players from the fans. She needed to talk with Bill Potter.

The Men from Dancing Deer were playing in the field and the Hotshots had runners on first and second. Bill and a woman in a pretty yellow sundress were sitting on the player's bench.

"Mr. Potter . . . yoo-hoo, Mr. Potter."

Bill looked over his shoulder through the chained links. He turned, took another look at the playing field, and then walked to Mr. Ridley's granddaughter.

"Yes, ma'am. Nothing wrong with Mr. Ridley I hope."

"No. He's about the same. He told me to bring you this." She picked up an old brown bat she had leaned against the fence. "My great-grandfather whittled this on his front porch while a mid-wife birthed my grandfather. He later sanded it smooth and boned the wood. I don't know what that means, but it was important enough to grandfather that he wanted me to mention it to you.

173

"He said it has one hit left in it and for you to give it to Bear Radisson. He said Bear needs to take a few practice swings because the bat isn't made of ash but of chestnut. It's heavier. It weighs . . . m'mm, let me think . . . oh yes, it weighs forty-six ounces. I don't know why that's important either. I do know that this was the only bat grandfather used during his entire career with Pittsburgh. And he only used it in games. Never in batting practice. He also never let anyone else bat with it until now."

Bill took the bat. "Thank you, ma'am. We can sure use that one hit. Bear's hit into three double-plays so far."

There was a loud crack of the bat and Bill looked away to see a Hotshot runner cross the plate. He looked back to tell Adelle to take a seat and watch the rest of the game, but she had already left. She now walked fast to sit with her grandfather for the final inning.

In the bottom of the seventh, Paul Nelson struck out, Amos was thrown out short to first, and Wally popped to third. The Men from Dancing Deer hadn't scored a run since the second inning. Now that Harriet couldn't tell them when a fast ball was coming, they were off-balance, unable to decide if the ball thrown was a fastball or a curve.

Going into the top of the eighth, the Hotshots had closed the gap and were now down by a single run. The Men from Dancing Deer were sinking fast. They didn't think they could hit the Hotshot's pitcher. The boys in blue suffocated in a dismal funk.

The Hotshots scored another run in the top of the eighth, tying the game at six. In the bottom of that same inning, Daniel walked and Leonard singled to right field but was picked off by the pitcher when he strayed too far from the bag. David Blaine flied to center and Abner went down swinging.

In the top of the ninth, the Hotshot's center fielder hit a ball deep in the hole and Daniel Poul made a lunging grab, but had a long throw from his knees and couldn't get enough on it to catch the speedster flying to first. The next batter sacrificed him to second and he came in on a single to left.

When the Men from Dancing Deer came to bat in the bottom of the ninth they had lost the lead. Now the Hotshots were in the driver's seat with a one-run lead at seven to six. This was Dancing Deer's last chance, and their chances of pulling the upset looked bleak. The bottom of the order was due up and no one had been able to make decent contact with the ball for the last six innings.

Jed struck out on the unhittable, uncatchable pitch but managed to run to first while James Paul scrambled after the ball.

In the bleachers a pretty lady in a short brown bob saw that it was Bear's time to bat. She crossed her fingers. He'd already been thrown out in three double-plays. Now Jed was at first and Bear had a fourth opportunity. How devastating to his ego another double-play would be. She closed her eyes and whispered, "Come on Bear. You can do this. I'm here for you."

From the radio Mr. Ridley and the two women listened as Jesse gave them each event as it happened.

"It looks like Bill Potter's going to pinch-hit for Bear Radisson. Bear has had a rough time of it today. He's been in three double-plays. Bill picks up a bat and takes a practice swing. He hands the bat to Bear. Bear's getting another chance. They're talking. I guess Bill's giving some last minute instructions. Mr. Ridley . . . Mr. Ridley, they're looking at your bat. He takes a practice swing and another. Bear slowly, solemnly walks to home plate. It's as if he thinks he has a job to do. Jed takes his lead at first. He's the tying run, but not much of a stealing danger. The pitcher winds, comes to set, looks to first, kicks, and throws home. The ball's low and away. Ball one.

"Bear steps out, takes a practice swing. Takes another. And another. He's back in the box. Waggles the bat, takes it back, and waits. The pitcher kicks and comes home. Low in the dirt. Ball two. A walk gets the runner in scoring position for Amos and Wally. Jed waits at first wearing a blue warm-up jacket.

"Bear raises his right hand, asking for time. He steps out of the batter's box. He's looking at something on the bat. He runs his hand down the length of the bat from the barrel to the handle. He's saying something to it. Mr. Ridley, he's talking to your bat. Now he grips the bat with both hands and takes a slow swing—all the way around. He steps back into the batter's box. Holding the bat in his left hand, his right extends level with the ground back toward the umpire palm facing out. He extends the bat waist high over the plate. He then reaches out

175

with the bat still in his left hand and points to center field. Bear grips the bat with both hands and takes it back high over his shoulder, his feet close together. The pitcher starts his wind-up, comes to set, looks to first, Jed's got a short lead, the pitcher kicks, and comes to home."

Bear waits on the pitch. He starts his swing. His left foot strides toward the mound. The bat comes around led by his left elbow, the bat makes solid contact with the ball and his wrists break so the bat can extend on around as his torso coils at the waist. His weight transfers at the moment of impact from the back foot to the front. A loud crack. Jesse heard it. The fans heard it. Julius heard it. Even the three people in Mr. Ridley's bedroom heard it.

"Holy cow. Bear's hit the ball to deep center—where he pointed. The center fielder looks up, turns, and runs. He looks back over his shoulder, stops, looks up, and watches the flight of the ball. He's now heading in. Holy cow! Bear Radisson has hit the ball into downtown Dancing Deer. Dancing Deer wins, eight to seven."

CHAPTER 31 – HARRIET'S WINNINGS

Adelle held her grandfather's hand. She saw the smile spread across his face when the loud crack came through the speakers.

He knew it was a homerun long before anyone else. Jesse said the ball was still ascending its arc when it passed over the center fielder's head. Mr. Ridley knew what it looked like, even though he had his eyes closed.

In the background, in the far reaches of his hearing, Mr. Ridley heard his fans yelling, "Yea, Sugar Bear." The crowd's noise reverberated throughout the stadium. The stomping of feet punctuated their yells of "Sugar Bear, Sugar Bear."

Mr. Ridley rounded first and started a slow trot around the remaining bases. Confetti streamed onto the field, an organ played through large speakers, fans poured onto the field and ran alongside, his buddies waited at home to jump on his back. By his side a woman he often saw in dreams said, "You did good, Torguson. Now it's time to come home. I've been waiting for you. We've all been waiting for you."

Through the cacophony he could faintly hear. "Grandfather . . . oh, no. Nurse come quick. I think he's going. Grandfath . . ."

Back at the ball field there was pandemonium as the fans jumped to their feet yelling at the top of their lungs. several people did not yell. Two busses of people from Skunk Hollow and nine men from Dancing Deer were not happy at all.

Mayor Bob turned to Harold Greenleaf. "I can't believe Bill did it to us again."

"You might be sunk, but I'm glad the Peckerwoods won. I covered my cash bet with some people from Skunk Hollow and won't mind paying Bill in the least. Bob, you should probably start looking for a new line of work. Ha, ha."

The Men from Dancing Deer shook hands with the New York Hotshots. Harriet, Bill, and Julius talked near third base.

Julius asked Harriet, "How were you able to figure out our signals?"

She shrugged, "A scouting report said your pitcher shook his glove before he threw the fastball. We didn't know any other signs."

"Well, that was enough. Is your man's arm all right? It didn't look like it affected his pitching that much."

"We'll get it on ice after the celebrating settles down. Actually it was his right arm that got hit not his left. Where you heading next?"

"California. We got a few days off, then we play a team in Sacramento. Do you think any of your boys would want to join us? We have about twenty more games before we finish the year in Kansas City. Our last game is against the Kansas City Monarchs—Satchel Page and company."

Bill spoke up for the first time. "How would we go about getting tickets for that game?"

"I'll send you some. How many you need? Ten? Twenty?"

"I'd like to bring the players and their families—all the ones you leave behind. I'll have a busload. Could you get me sixty? I'll be happy to pay."

"No problem. I'll send sixty. But I'm only interested in four of your players: third, short, first, and your wonderful pitcher."

"Paul Nelson plays third. He's a salesman for a candy company and has a family. Short is Daniel Poul. He's single and foot-loose. And first—the big guy—his name is Bear Radisson. He's also single. You might be able to talk both of those guys into joining up. The pitcher is in his forties and married. He owns a farm with a small herd of cattle. He might be interested, but I doubt it."

Harriet spoke up again. "Mr. Mosivido."

"Call me Julius."

"Julius, come join us for supper. We have a big celebration party planned, complete with a band. Our treat. We've blocked off Main Street in front of the hotel and moved out serving tables."

Julius reached into his pocket. He pulled out a dirty envelope and handed it to Bill. Here is the two thousand you won. I'm also donating the gate and concessions. I want you to use it to do something nice for your citizens. They've treated us like we were family." Julius turned facing Harriet, "Ma'am, I'm afraid if I stay for the celebration my players will abandon ship and ask for jobs. I have a woman who's already thinking of taking her money and opening a millinery store in your pretty little town. No, we better be on our way. I just want to talk to those men before I go. Thank you for asking though. Oh, and that mayor of yours needs to relocate to Chicago. I believe he's out of place in Dancing Deer."

"Ha, ha, we agree."

That evening everyone who was anyone was in front of the Ritz Grand Hotel and Ballroom. On an outside podium Bill gave a speech. Harriet would have been carried around on the shoulders of her players had she not insisted that it was not very ladylike, and besides, she was wearing a dress. Katy said she wouldn't mind, and Bear Radisson lifted her high in the air and kissed her full on the lips.

He said, "Kate, I'm so happy." He twirled her around in a circle. "Here." He started to put her down. "Let me get you something to drink."

"That's all right, just hold me like this for awhile."

A tall slender woman with a short bob hairdo placed her drink on a table and walked away. Faye put her hand on Bear's shoulder. "Katy, I'll be leaving in the morning. I've got to go find W.W."

Bear eased his grip and let Katy slide to the ground. Her feet had been suspended two feet above the pavement. Katy said, "I thought he was coming here."

"He was. He was coming to get me. We were going to get married. But his train had an accident. He fell into a river trying to save a little girl and was swept away. They haven't found his body. They sent a search party but gave up looking after a few days. He's out there, cold, shivering, hurt. I'm going after him."

"I'll come too."

"No." She looked at Bear Radisson, then at Katy. "You stay here. I'll go check things out. I'll call after I decide what to do. I may want you to bring a few people with you. W.W. belongs to Dancing Deer and I think she'll want him back as much as I do."

Someone yelled out, "The New York Hotshots have pulled their bus up to the barricade. Let's invite them to join us."

Judge McAdams slapped Daniel Poul on his back, then gave a gentle shove as he said, "Do us proud, boy."

Daniel ran through the celebrants. "They're waiting on me. I'm going to bat against Satchel Page in October. Everybody come to Kansas City." He was down the street in a flash, carrying a suitcase with clothes sticking out from every corner.

Bill took Harriet's hand. "That leaves you and me, Babe. What reward do you want for winning the game?"

"I want you."

The End

Author Bio

Ron Lambert, an examined life

As an accountant in a small West Texas town, I spend my days studying the bank statements and tax returns of other people's businesses. I classify, summarize, and display their financial transactions in some meaningful format. I love creating order out of chaos.

I'm middle-aged and twice married—with the second blessed from heaven. Four grown children, their children, two bobbing tails of barking energy, and one sly cat round out my cache of treasure.

Over the years I have owned and operated two boutique retail stores, several service businesses, one ranch, and one restaurant. I have been prosperous and poor, with wild fluctuations in between. At present, being neither rich nor poor, I consider my status as deeply entrenched in middle class—a term bandied about by politicians and economists.

A few years ago, in an effort to restore my youth, I purchased an old sofa on two wheels. Since that initial existential groping, I have occasionally strapped sacks of clothes, maps, and a compass that doesn't seem to work onto the back cushion. After kissing my wife, I set out for adventure and story and to find answers to the big questions. Usually, after only a week or so, I realize what I left behind was more important than what I set out to find and drive a day and a night hell-bent-for-leather back home.

I then settle into an old and comfortable routine. I read a few books, attend a few plays, daydream of new horizons, and plan my next adventure. I kept a journal on my first excursion. It was such an exhilarating experience: rewriting the journal and incorporating the pictures I took that I became intoxicated to the point I wrote a novel.

At present, with pen on fire, I am writing my eighth book. I'll win prestigious awards and be asked to speak at the local library if someone would read what I have written.

If you're looking for an evening spent with colorful and mesmerizing characters, if you want to immerse yourself in a rollicking good story, enthrall yourself to the point of madness, go two days without bathing, then have I got a story for you.

Additional Novels
The Dancing Deer Story

Soon all will be available in multiple formats at Amazon.com and www.printersguildpublishing.com Trade Paperbacks in perfect binding can be purchased at our corporate office and from display stands in several of our fine businesses in Columbus, Texas

Dancing Deer (Book 1)

Dancing Deer is the embodiment of small-town America. When asked, she sent her sons to war. This is the story of The Calhoun—one of those boys. It's also about his fellow combatants, the men he served, the men he fought, and the women he loved.

There is the French Resistance, the German Gestapo, *Midge at the Mike*, Anzio Annie, the *Gustav Line*, and the US Army's Forty-Fifth Infantry campaigning from Sicily through Italy, France, and Germany to push back the formidable Germans. But this story is so much more.

Find a comfortable chair and settle in with a great new book. You won't be disappointed.

The Last Dance (Book 2)

Bill Potter is charged with murdering his Friday night squeeze. His bumbling lawyer steps out of a dead-end job of contracts and leases to save Bill from being strapped to "Old Spanky." Bill's wife returns after a twenty year absence to muddy the waters and it's up to her and Pepe, the womanizing Resistance fighter and WWI spy from France, to solve the case.

The Measure of a Man (Book 3)

A group of Cuban immigrants decide to barnstorm the Midwest by entertaining the towns they come to with a game of ball. When they get to Dancing Deer the men on the city council con Bill Potter into a wager for more than they can afford to lose. Bill's position is that the Men from Dancing Deer will prevail. With a team of misfits and one win under their belts, Bill goes searching for a new manager. His ex-wife is traveling throughout the Western US with Pepe, the French womanizer. She knows more about ball than anyone and he has to convince her to come back and once again save him from the wolves at the door.

Lost in Appalachia (Book 4)

Dancing Deer's Chief of Police is lost in the mountains of West Virginia. Suffering from an injury, he can't remember who he is or why he's lost. Two kids take him in and hide him from a determined fiancée. The chief of police is in the process of teaching the kids how to read when the fiancée posts a big reward for knowledge of his whereabouts. The chief thinks he must have committed a major crime for someone to pony up such a large bounty. With the children hiding him, the chief has to decide what to do when he learns the shady secrets of an earlier life.

Christmas in Dancing Deer (Book 5)

St. Bartholomew's is consolidating its orphanage, but the children don't want to be separated. They come up with an alternative plan to present to the church, but the women of Dancing Deer bring the orphan girls into their homes for the holidays. The orphan boys leave on their own in the snow three days before Christmas and spend a night with a burdened bank robber in a desolated cabin. This is a classic tale of how good triumphs over evil in an adult setting.

Beggarman, Thief (Book 6)

A story of a bank robber who finds his moment of epiphany in a shack with six lost little boys. He goes home after twenty years on the lamb to have Christmas with his family and to right his wrongs. But he finds his past is in hot pursuit and the new life he has found is in jeopardy. He runs away in the clutches of a pretty lady evangelist who is taking her show on the road to the very town where he committed his last crime. This is a wonderful story that can be enjoyed by everyone.

Toe to Toe with A Drunken Philosopher

This is really one story in three parts. First we have the high school philosophy teacher who has to resign his position much as Aristotle had to when the authorities in Athens came looking for him.

Part number two is of an indigent Irish family who emigrate from the Emerald Isle. The little Irish boy in the family grows up to become a priest.

Then the third part pits the philosopher and the priest in a contest of wits.

Racing the Wind (Book 7 in the series, but not yet finished)

The story of a boy with plans to someday build bridges or design skyscrapers. He decides to start with a racer in the All American Soapbox Derby. Problems, orchestrated by his main adversary, creep into the racer's production. The boy has to rely on the help of a fellow classmate—a girl—to find the source of his problems and to finish the racer and the race.

Order Form

Book Name	Qty	Price	Extension
Dancing Deer	☐	$17.95	_____
The Last Dance	☐	$15.95	_____
The Measure of a Man	☐	$15.95	_____
Lost in Appalachia	☐	$15.95	_____
Christmas in Dancing Deer	☐	$15.95	_____
Beggarman, Thief	☐	$15.95	_____
Toe to Toe with a Drunken Philosopher	☐	$15.95	_____
Racing the Wind	☐	$15.95	_____

Sub-Total _____

Sales Tax (for Texas purchases) @ 8.25% _____
Shipping: $4.00 for 1st Book
$2.00 for each Additional _____

Grand Total _____

Would you like your book(s) autographed? **Yes** ☐ **No** ☐

Would you like your book(s) wrapped? **Yes** ☐ **No** ☐

To_____ **From**_____

Order Form (continued)

Name _____

Shipping Address:

    Military APO   _____

    Street or PO Box   _____

    State and Zip   _____

Telephone   _____

Payment:

    Check Enclosed   ☐

    Credit Card:

        Discover   ☐

        Visa   ☐

        MasterCard   ☐

Card Number   _____

Expiration Date   _____

Code (on back)   _____

Keep Credit Card Information for future purchases   ☐

Order Form (instructions)

Boxes   Place quantity or checkmark (X) where applicable

Mail Completed Form To:
Printers Guild Publishing House, llc
425 Spring Street, Suite 101
Columbus, Texas 78934-2461

Or Fax Form to:
(979) 733-0015

Or Call-In Your Order during business hours:
(979) 732-2962

For Pick-Up:
You are welcome to come by our office in the Stafford Opera House at 425 Spring Street, Suite 101, Columbus, Texas to pick up your order and save shipping costs or to talk with the author.

Please call (979) 732-2962 to make sure someone will be there.

Security
We do not share any of your information with anyone. We do not keep your credit card information unless you check the box allowing us to do so for future purchases.